OLO OF THE MOUND BUILDERS

by

Jo Ann Harter

Bloomington, IN  Milton Keynes, UK

AuthorHouse™
1663 Liberty Drive, Suite 200
Bloomington, IN 47403
www.authorhouse.com
Phone: 1-800-839-8640

AuthorHouse™ UK Ltd.
500 Avebury Boulevard
Central Milton Keynes, MK9 2BE
www.authorhouse.co.uk
Phone: 08001974150

This book is a work of fiction. People, places, events, and situations are the product of the author's imagination. Any resemblance to actual persons, living or dead, or historical events, is purely coincidental.

© 2007 Jo Ann Harter. All rights reserved.

No part of this book may be reproduced, stored in a retrieval system, or transmitted by any means without the written permission of the author.

First published by AuthorHouse 7/30/2007

ISBN: 978-1-4343-1079-8 (sc)

Library of Congress Control Number: 2007903479

Printed in the United States of America
Bloomington, Indiana

This book is printed on acid-free paper.

A portion of the royalties from this book will benefit the Archaeological Conservancy, the only national nonprofit organization that identifies, acquires, and preserves the most significant archaeological sites in the United States.

WHY SAVE ARCHAEOLOGICAL SITES?

The ancient people of North America left virtually no written records of their cultures. Clues that might someday solve the mysteries of prehistoric America are still missing, and when a ruin is destroyed by looters, or leveled for a shopping center, precious information is lost. By permanently preserving endangered ruins, we make sure they will be here for future generations to study and enjoy.

Line drawings by Jo Ann Harter

ACKNOWLEDGEMENTS

In the process of writing *Olo Of The Mound* Builders I consulted hundreds of books, journals, and articles related to the many facets of Native American life in A.D.1,000. At Ball State University in Muncie, Indiana, Ronald Hicks, Ph.D., served as my first and finest advisor on archaeology. Help came from many directions in the writing of *Olo Of The Mound Builders*. I am grateful to Howard Denson and North Florida Writers, who provided encouragement and critiques. Other friends have helped in countless ways. I am grateful to Tom Goodsite for his advice and his comprehensive knowledge of stuttering. My gratitude goes to my treasured friends, Doris Cass, Phyllis Rowland, and Pamela Murray, who were first to hear every word I wrote. And I wish to extend sincere appreciation to Caryn Suarez, of Promoting Outstanding Writers, who opened my eyes to the complexities and strengths of publishing and marketing. I am most grateful to my son-in-law, Bill Tappan, who taught me computer skills and was ever ready to help with my problems. Sincere thanks go to my three children: Pamela, who used every opportunity to assist me and encourage my work. George, who enthusiastically accompanied me to Cahokia Mounds State Historic Site in Illinois. And Matthew, who encouraged me with his understanding of primitive tools, and who brought me a slab of red ochre, balls of yellow ocbre, and the priceless nutting stone.

And finally, my heartfelt gratitude to my three grandsons for lending me their names:

        Wade -- <u>EDAW</u>
        Sam -- Te <u>MAS</u> ah
        Dan -- <u>NAD</u> o mas.

FOREWORD

Olo of the Mound Builders is a story set in prehistoric North America in the Mississippian Era, A.D. 700 to A.D. 1500. Clusters of mounds bordered nearly every major waterway. Once proud examples of Native American ingenuity, these mounds now serve as humble state parks. They stand as silent reminders of the past.

Olo of the Mound Builders is an adventure story with vivid characters, settings rich in history and a sense of place. This story makes unusual demands on the imagination. An author once said, "Imagine that a squirrel on the Atlantic coast could jump from tree to tree and never stop until it reached the Mississippi River." Imagine no cities, only small villages, no highways, only trails through the forests, no light except from the sun and the moon, and imagine that everyone had brown hair, brown eyes, and copper colored skin.

Olo lived in this world.

CHAPTER 1

AT THE CRACKLE of footsteps on twigs, Olo looked up. He shielded his eyes from the sun's glare and looked toward the woods. He saw movement and heard voices.

"L-L-Look! E-E-Enemy!" He shouted.

The workers looked up, laughed at him, then returned to their work.

"N-No! L-Look!" He screamed, pointing to the treeline. "E-Enemy!"

Shouts sounded from the trees. Other workers harvesting tobacco, looked up to see hostile warriors swarming out of the nearby woods with spears flashing and war clubs raised. Fierce shouts and whoops filled the air as they rushed onto the field. Everyone ran.

He dropped his bundle and ran away. The wind blew past him as his legs pumped. He felt a thud on the back of his head, and his head jerked forward. As he bit his lip, his mouth felt wet and warm.

He saw bright stars, then blackest night surrounded him as he fell to the ground.

When he came to, standing over him was a short boy with angry, dark eyes. He ordered him to get up and jabbed him with the point of his spear.

He staggered to his feet. The salty taste of blood made him gag. His head pounded with pain. He put his hand to his head, it came away bloody. He felt lightheaded in the hot autumn sun as he and the others were herded into a group.

His heart raced and his hands trembled as he and the workers were forced to lie face down while warriors tied rope around their necks, six prisoners to a group. When they were ordered to stand up, they could walk, but escape by running was impossible. Both the workers and the tobacco harvest were captured.

His throat closed in fear. "W-Where are we going?"

The warriors gestured with their spears and shouted, "Form a line!"

He was happy he understood their words. He picked up a bundle of tobacco and fell into line with the others.

The country was flat and heavily wooded. For two days the warriors marched their captives west toward the sunset. On the third day, they turned south. The quiet, uneventful march followed a wide, well-worn trail through the woods. The weather was mild and the autumn sun was warm.

His head hurt. He figured that because he was taller and bigger, they gave him a heavier load. The headband of the burden-strap dug into his forehead like a knife. To forget the pain, he tried to remember his mother's face.

His mother had gone to the Great Maker five winters ago. When he closed his eyes, he could not see her face… why had she left him without even a vision of her?

Since his mother had no brothers or sisters, he had been adopted by a large family. He had learned to keep quiet, stay out of the way, or he would be mistreated.

But already he knew they wouldn't miss him. He had heard tales. Raiding for captives was common and some captives were treated so well, they never wanted to return to their own village.

The trail ended at the edge of the woods on a hill. Below them lay open fields. On the distant horizon huge mounds rose majestically into the sky surrounded by the houses of a village.

He stopped. He had never seen anything so big. "L-Look!" Olo shouted with excitement, "T-There they are!"

Olo saw the chief's house atop an earthen pyramid at one end of the village while a temple topped another pyramid at the opposite end. A smaller mound was under construction. Excitement raced through the crew as they got their first glimpse of the huge mounds.

Everyone stopped to stare at the view and exclaim how big and impressive the mounds were.

Olo stood gazing at the sight before him. *There is our destination--our new home.* The warriors marched their captives across the open field. As they drew nearer, the mounds seemed to grow. He could not take his eyes off the sight. *"L-Look how big they are!"*

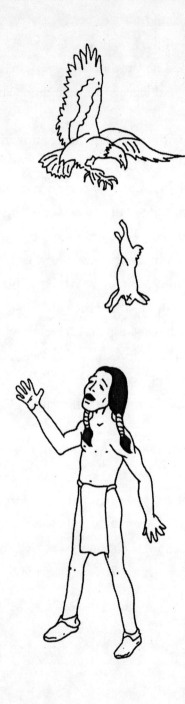

CHAPTER 2

THE MOUNDS WERE flat topped pyramids with steeply sloping sides covered with grass. A smaller mound, under construction, stood at the edge of the village. Olo counted six conical mounds and two ridge-top mounds.

I've never seen such a big village. Olo walked on, his eyes on the horizon.

He pulled up short to avoid bumping into the man in front of him who had stopped and was looking up.

In the sky, an eagle glided around and around. It made two circles, then folded its wings in a steep dive toward earth. The eagle reappeared with a small rabbit in its talons. The rabbit writhed, twisted and turned, freeing itself from the eagle's claws, it plunged down toward the band of men crossing the field.

The other men dropped their tobacco bundles and covered their heads with their hands. Olo dropped his bundle, raised his arms and caught the rabbit. The limp body and eyes that gazed sightlessly, straight ahead, told him the rabbit had given up its spirit.

"It is d-dead, probably from fright."

Shouts rang out as other warriors ran over. Excitedly, the guards all talked at once. "This is an omen before our eyes."

"The chiefs should be told this captive is a chosen one."

"We might invite a curse. I'm of the Bird Clan, are you?"

"We are in danger if we disobey the eagle's wishes."

"This is an omen." Everyone agreed.

Olo stood very still. *What is wrong? What are they saying? Did I do wrong to catch the eagle's food?*

Sharp commands rang out. A guard took the dead rabbit from Olo and dropped it into a small bag. The band continued their march. This time the excited guards urged their captives to a faster pace. As they approached the village, Olo saw carved, wooden effigies of deer, turtles, and eagles on the largest building's roof ridge.

Why do those buildings look so special? Maybe priests or chiefs live there--or do they worship the Great Spirit up there closer to the sky?

The path led beside a deep ditch, a dry moat, bordered on the other side by a defensive palisade. A tall fence, made of upright logs daubed with clay, towered over them.

An enemy would have a hard time climbing over that fence, Olo thought.

When they came to a bridge over the ditch, Olo could see other guards opening a heavy gate in the fence. They entered and walked between fences on each side until the path opened into a large plaza where children played and women worked. Smoke filled the air from many cooking fires with stew pots suspended over them. Good smells of roasting venison met Olo's nostrils.

Food smells good--I am hungry. Olo's stomach rumbled in answer to his thoughts.

Abruptly they were ordered to stop. The guards motioned Olo apart from the others. The short, frowning guard who captured Olo, was ordered to take Olo's tobacco bundle. His face darkened and he scowled even more as he grumbled and staggered under the load. He and the others continued their march and disappeared behind a mound.

Other armed guards untied the rope from his neck and tied his hands behind his back. Walking one on each side, they escorted him across the busy plaza. The white chert tip of the guards's lance, urged Olo up squared steps of red cedar placed in the steep ramp of the great mound.

Olo's legs trembled and felt strangely numb as he stepped up. His mouth was dry. *What will happen to me?*

"Stand still," the guard ordered when they reached the top. Olo took a deep breath of clean air. He could see a great distance over the city. He was awed by the view of the surrounding countryside that seemed to stretch forever.

I can see the path opening in the woods on my right and there is the bend of the river on the left.

Time passed. Olo stood between the two guards. A hot wind blew against his face. His head pounded.

I wish I could shield my eyes from the sun. The ropes cut into his wrists and his chin trembled.

As his heartbeat quickened, standing there in the sunlight, he felt tears well up in his throat. *No! I will not cry.* He swallowed hard.

Olo felt fear crawling up the back of his neck. *I'm in big trouble.*

Long minutes passed. Olo heard flies buzzing. The guards nudged him forward. He walked from the bright light through the open door of the council house. He stepped over the threshold. Gradually his vision adjusted to the gloom inside. Sunlight coming through the smoke hole in the roof, made twilight rather than darkness.

What will they do to me? Olo's heart pounded with fear.

CHAPTER 3

OLO SAW PLASTERED walls with intricate designs painted on the white clay. He recognized a red spiral painted on the wall. The flickering light from a firebowl placed before it, made the spiral turn and twist, and made him blink.

From a distance Olo heard faint drum beats. The scent of tobacco mixed with fragrant hickory smoke filled the air.

One guard remained at the door while the other led Olo forward. He untied Olo's wrists and placed the dead rabbit in Olo's hands.

Olo found himself standing inside a circle of seated men. Three men sat on a platform higher than the others. *Elders and chiefs, leaders of this village*, Olo guessed.

The guard had their full attention as he told the story, how the eagle dropped its prey and how Olo caught it, how they saw it as an omen and dared not offend the eagle, totem of the Bird Clan.

Olo looked into the wrinkled face of the elderly chief seated in the center. He had a carved, wooden staff in his hand. His shoulder length gray hair was pinned on top of his head with copper pins and an owl's wing spread out behind his topknot. Copper ear spools filled each ear lobe. A palm sized stone gorget hung around his neck. Black tattoos adorned his face and his gaze was stern and solemn as he listened.

I am thankful the voices are not angry. Olo breathed a sigh.

There was much discussion between the leaders. Each man had something to say and at times everyone talked at once. A hush came over the room. In absolute silence they all turned their attention to the door. The head shaman of the organized priesthood approached. Olo felt their awe and reverence for him.

His long white braids fell over the shoulders of the old man's robe. A polished shell gorget hung from his neck and copper ear spools glinted in his earlobes. He moved with slow dignity and the way he held his head proudly erect gave him more the air of a chief than a shaman.

Olo saw a man of many seasons. His old walnut face was lined with deep grooves. One eye was completely covered with a white, milky cloud and a smaller cloud grew on the other eye. A tattoo like a blackbird in flight, covered his forehead over his white eyebrows.

His thin lips parted in a grimace and his voice was harsh. He turned toward Olo. "I am Temasah. Your story sticks in my mind like a splinter."

He produced a small bag. From it he scattered corn meal to the four directions: north, east, south and west. He glanced heavenward and then downward, then bowed to the north, east, south and west, acknowledging the Six Sacred Persons who controlled the winds. Turning to the assembled group, he held his hands, palms up, as he prayed, "Let my words ride on the wind and fly to the ear of the Great Spirit."

"Share my vision," he said looking at them as he sat down.

Temasah's chin settled on his chest. His eyes stared into space. He began to chant in a husky voice. Long minutes passed before he spoke. Olo wondered if he had fallen asleep.

"I see a copper mask of the long-nosed-god. The fog plays tricks... first it is the face of the long-nosed-god, then it is this solemn face. What does this vision say to me? Why do I see this face? Does the eagle totem speak to me?" His words faded back into the chant, then silence.

Temasah opened his eyes. He stood erect and spoke in a strong voice. "Experience, knowledge and wisdon only come with age. Youth requires direction and guidance. I am in need of an apprentice. Age needs to be rejuvenated by youth. Could we not place this young man on probation for a time to judge his merits, to test his worth, and determine for ourselves if indeed he is the eagle's chosen one?"

They pondered this information for several minutes. Then an elder spoke. "Age and youth need each other. Is not the eagle the totem of the Bird Clan? And should we not heed the eagle's choice? Would a curse be placed on us if the council does not honor the eagle's wish?"

The discussion that followed was brief. The chief banged the butt end of his staff on the ground four times. "The council has been heard. The captive will be apprenticed to the shaman, Temasah."

Olo's shoulders relaxed and he exhaled . He realized he had been holding his breath. *They will not punish me*, he thought.

CHAPTER 4

TEMASAH FOUND OLO'S arm. "I need help walking down the steps. What is your name?"

Olo looked down at his feet and answered in a small voice, "O-Olo, sir."

A guard appeared on Temasah's other side. Together they descended the steps. The guard escorted them across the plaza to the shaman's lodge. At the doorway he bade them good-night and was gone.

Temasah and Olo entered the lodge. Olo noticed tied bundles of herbs, roots and flowers hanging from the rafters. A sweet smell filled the air. An old woman appeared and took the dead rabbit from Olo's hands.

Out of the shadows, a white dog bounded up to them. Olo stood very still while the dog sniffed him. *Is he friend or foe?* Olo hardly breathed. Just then the dog lay on his back in total submission at Olo's feet.

Olo squatted and ran his hands over the silky, white fur. The dog wiggled in delight as Olo felt his cold nose, his soft ears and his warm belly. Olo spoke for the first time. "Sir, w-what do you call him?"

"Edaw," Temasah answered. "The dog's name is Edaw."

The old woman appeared to help him sit down on a platform covered with soft skins. "This is my wife, Annawa," Temasah said.

She glanced at Olo and nodded.

Temasah tried to remove his robe but his hands were like injured birds looking for a place to roost. Annawa removed his robe. She disappeared into the shadows and returned with bear grease to massage his fingers to ease the pain.

"I am the keeper of the white dog. Have you not heard that legend?" Temasah said.

"N-No, sir, please tell me," Olo replied sitting down in front of him. The dog curled up at Olo's side.

Temasah took a deep breath and began. "We believe dog is the faithful one, the guide who personifies courage. In the ceremony, a white dog is sacrificed and his spirit carries messages to the Great Spirit."

Olo's heart jumped when he heard the word sacrifice but he said nothing.

The old wife, gray hair tumbling over her withered face, appeared and set food before them. She urged them to eat. In thanks, Olo touched the back of her wrinkled hand. She looked up. She smiled in response and stepped back into the shadows. They ate in silence. Olo was very hungry.

When the vessels were removed, the shaman ordered, "Move closer, Olo, so I can see you better." He talked to himself as he examined Olo. "He is taller than most boys. He is very thin. Perhaps his large frame carries the body of a future athlete." Taking Olo's hands in his, he felt Olo's long fine boned fingers.

"Stand up," he ordered. Olo stood. The shaman stood and took Olo's face in his hands and brought it close to his face. He mumbled, "A tall stoop-shouldered boy with a thin face and a long nose. But his dark eyes look calm and intelligent."

"How old are you?" Temasah said.

"I have s-seen thirteen w-winters, Sir."

Looking away, as if lost in thought, Temasah said, "Are the spirits working in Olo causing him to stutter?" Temasah said almost under his breath. He turned, "We will begin your lessons tomorrow. Goodnight." He walked into the darkness of the house.

Annawa indicated where Olo should sleep, and handed him a soft deerskin blanket. Olo's tired body cried out for rest. Edaw curled up beside him. As Olo drifted off, he felt the softness of Edaw's fur, the warmth of the dog's body. Just before he fell asleep, he saw his mother's face smiling at him through a fog.

CHAPTER 5

NEXT MORNING AFTER their meal, Temasah asked Olo to sit before him and remain quiet.

"I usually pray in silence, but this morning I will speak my prayer, because you need to learn how to pray." Temasah said.

"Oh, Great Spirit, hear my prayer. I have survived into old age, but now my eyesight grows dim. I am much in need of an apprentice. I long to pass on my knowledge of healing herbs, soothing potions and prayers--which prayer is best for a headache, which best for a broken bone."

Temasah's shoulders sagged. In a voice heavy with sorrow he said, "My heart aches as I remember my son, Yarrum, who has gone to be with you, Great Maker. I taught him everything I knew but I could not save him when he had the coughing sickness."

"Each time I look into Olo's solemn dark eyes, I am reminded of Yarrum and my heart breaks into pieces. He is with you now and I have been given a second chance."

"The eagle Spirit gave his food to Olo knowing it was the answer to my prayer. If that isn't enough proof, Edaw, the white dog, went to Olo and has never left his side... what more proof could I want? Thank you for answering my prayers."

The old man's shoulders hunched, making him appear frail and decrepit. Temasah opened his eyes and spoke to Olo, "You will spend each day learning the ways of a shaman. In the woods, I will teach you where to find bark, roots, and herbs needed to make medicine. I will teach you the prayers to honor the spirits so they will restore balance between the earth and the health of the people. You are chosen for this honor. You are gifted, Olo. I have a sensing."

Temasah summoned his wife. "You also must work every day. You and Edaw will carry water to the mound builders. Annawa will show you how this is done. You must keep one thought in your mind all day. As you work, remember these words: A good shaman hears with his heart as well as with his ears."

Annawa, Edaw, and Olo walked to a stand of trees at the edge of the plaza. There in the shade they set about making a harness, or travois, so Edaw could carry water from the spring to the mound builders laboring under the hot sun.

They cut strips of rawhide from a deerskin. Edaw stood still while they fitted the rawhide together to make the harness. Long hickory poles were fitted into the harness so he could drag a vessel filled with water on the platform between the two poles.

Olo, his head down, in a soft voice asked, "What should I call you?"

Also in a quiet voice, she answered, "Call me Mother."

Olo looked into her eyes and his heart quickened.

Later as Olo was cutting and braiding rawhide strips, he heard voices. He turned to see several boys laughing and pointing toward him.

"Oh, look here! See the chosen one! See, he is learning to work like a squaw," shouted the small warrior. "See how he works like a woman. And he s-s-stutters!" They ran away laughing.

Olo sat there with his heart in his throat.

"Nadac is a bad one. Heed them not," Annawa said.

Olo leaned forward, "Is that his name, Nadac? He captured me. He hit me on the head and knocked me down."

"A bad one," she replied.

They hooked Edaw up in the harness, walked to the spring, filled the vessel with water by dipping a gourd, then took the path to the mound under construction. The mound builders were happy to have fresh water to drink.

That night, after the evening meal, Olo sat very still, lost in thought. Temasah questioned, "Why is your face so long?"

Olo looked at his feet and mumbled, "I am b-burdened with b-bad thoughts."

"How so?" Temasah asked with a kind and gentle voice.

"I want to s-speak but something robs my mind. I always s-stutter," Olo lamented looking at the floor.

"Do not be troubled, I can cure that."

"You can?"

"Come sit before me and do exactly as I say. Look me full in the face. Look into my eyes. Take a slow, deep breath, then speak your mind. Do not be shy. Do this also each time you wish to speak."

"And that will cure me?" Olo whispered.

"Yes," Temasah said firmly. "Of that I am certain."

Annawa sat in the corner of the hut and seldom spoke. The corners of her eyes crinkled each time she looked at their new son. Olo's heart responded. He remembered the same look in his mother's eyes.

Lying on his pallet, staring at the smoldering embers in the firepit, *the Great Spirit has given me a new mother and father*, he thought, and fell asleep.

CHAPTER 6

OLO OPENED HIS eyes to see the morning sun shining through the smoke hole. Edaw greeted him with wet dog kisses on his face, neck and ears. He petted Edaw's head and stroked the fur on his back.

Temasah entered the room. "Take this from my hand and tell me what it is."

He took a small branch on which a fat caterpillar was eating the leaves. "I do not k-know, Sir, what is it?"

"A wonderment. A lesson. A surprise."

"This caterpillar is all that?"

"Put it in a safe place and watch. Something magical will happen." Temasah turned and walked away.

He stuck the branch securely into a crevice in the wall above his sleeping pallet. The fat caterpillar continued to eat the leaf.

"Whatever it is, I will watch it."

Later, Temasah, sitting on his fur pallet, said, "Before we begin the lesson, tell me about your family, your mother and father."

He sat, his chin on his chest. "M-my t-thoughts of Mother cut through my heart like a knife."

"I know," Temasah said. "Take a deep breath."

He saw a picture in his mind's eye. "I see a memory. Mother and I are standing on the river bank waving good-bye as we watch Father's canoe slip through the water. The sun is glinting off the ripples in the river."

He looked up. "The same sparkling river I love to swim in."

He continued. "Father was a trader. I remember watching him pack the little, clay, face-pipes into nests of grass in a deerskin, then tie the long, narrow bundle around his waist."

His chin went back to his chest and in a small voice, "M-many moons later when he never returned, Mother cried in the dark. Her tears fell in my hair and wet my forehead. He must have had an accident she whispered to me, or he would come home to us."

Tears slid down his cheeks. Edaw broke the spell as he licked the salty tears from Olo's face.

"And your mother?" Temasah asked in a soft voice.

"She went to the Great Maker five winters ago. She had the coughing sickness same as your son."

"What happened then?" Temasah asked.

"I c-could not speak for ten moons. When I again spoke, I stuttered. The chief gave me to a family with many children. We were all beaten and knocked about. My new sisters and brothers mocked me and laughed at me--the same way Nadac laughs at me."

"Nadac, the chief's son, laughs at you?"

"Y-yes. He captured me and teases me because I stutter and do women's work." Olo put his hands over his face in humiliation.

"Ah...." Temasah nodded with understanding.

Annawa appeared with Olo's daily cup of herbal tea and a soothing drink for the old shaman. She placed a basket of corn cakes and a clay pot filled with hickory butter in front of them. They ate in silence.

"Today you and Edaw will accompany Annawa to the clay hill. She is in need of new clay for her pots and effigy pipes. The beautiful autumn is to be enjoyed before Mother Earth is covered with snow." Temasah drew the cloak around his shoulders and departed.

Olo put the leather harness on Edaw and inserted the long hickory poles. Together they followed Annawa out an exit in the palisade nearest the river. Walking along a narrow path, they went to a place in the river bank where a yellow streak of clay lay between layers of darker soil.

"Quiet now," she commanded. Olo stood still and Edaw lay down at his feet.

"We must not dig clay from the earth without proper religious observances. The earth is our sacred mother. We depend on her for life and health."

She raised her hands, palms upward, and began to chant. Then she scattered corn meal to the wind. She turned to the north, east, south and west, making a complete circle.

With a mussel-shell hoe, Olo dug out all the clay. "This work is play. I like it. Do you enjoy this, Edaw?" Olo asked. Edaw wagged his tail in response.

Annawa stood by listening. "Alone with your work, you do not stutter, Olo."

"I h-had not noticed," Olo said.

"Pray to the Great Spirit. He will help you with your problems." Annawa helped him place the clay in a hide receptacle on the platform between the two poles. She tightened the rope on the load of clay, turned and climbed up the bank.

Olo helped Edaw pull the load up the river bank. When they were back on the path, Edaw could pull it himself.

Leaves on the trees had turned to red and gold, and there was a chill in the air. Olo, walking ahead of Edaw pulling the travois, felt something hit his head. He looked around and saw rocks being thrown from the nearby woods. He saw Nadac and several boys line up to throw rocks at him. One large rock hit Olo on the shoulder.

"Catch that, O, Chosen One." Nadac shouted.

Just then Edaw yelped in pain as a rock hit him in the head. He slumped down in his harness.

Olo ran to him and saw a red blood stain appear on the white fur on Edaw's head.

Olo felt his anger burst. His expression was set in grim lines. "Stop! Stop this now! Why do you taunt me?"

Annawa stood there shaking her walking stick at them. Laughing and jeering the boys turned and ran away into the woods.

Olo turned his attention to Edaw. "There, there, you only have a small cut on your head." Olo unhooked the travois and dragged it himself. Edaw walked free beside him.

When they returned to the lodge, Temasah taught Olo how to treat Edaw's wound. "Grind jimson-weed, mix with water to make a paste, then make a poultice and place it on the wound," Temasah instructed.

Olo was angry and his cheeks were bright as he retold the story. The words poured from his lips without hesitation.

"You did nothing to provoke them. You were right to defend yourself. Nadac is making cruel sport of you." Temasah comforted him.

That night, curled up on his sleeping skins, Olo whispered to Edaw, "Why is Nadac so angry with me? What have I done to cause this? I have done Nadac no wrong. Does he hate me just for being here?" There was hurt as well as anger in his voice.

Olo clenched his jaw until his teeth ached. "I will not cry. I will not." Edaw licked his hand until Olo fell asleep.

CHAPTER 7

THE NEXT DAY Olo noticed all the leaves were gone and the caterpillar had become a fat leaf hanging from a branch. Ten or twelve days passed. One morning when he looked at the twig stuck in the wall above his bed, he saw that the leaf had split open. A black-and-orange butterfly hung limply clinging to the old case.

He sat very still. "It's letting its wings dry," he whispered.

Temasah entered. Olo put up his finger to his lips then pointed to the butterfly.

Temasah smiled. "Put your finger next to it so it can sit on your finger."

He gently nudged the creature. It stepped onto his finger. Temasah motioned Olo to follow him. Outside, the newborn butterfly sensed the breeze, opened its wings for a moment, then flew away.

Temasah held his hands palms upward to the sky and prayed, "Fly to your fate as you help Mother Nature."

Turning to Olo, "Releasing a butterfly is a spiritual lesson. What did this teach you?"

Olo thought for several minutes. "The caterpillar rested in the leaf and changed into a beautiful butterfly."

"Yes, go on," Temasah urged.

"The worm needed food, a safe place to rest, while it was changing into a butterfly."

"Very good, Olo, and what else?"

"The Great Spirit makes all creatures. We watched the caterpillar change into a butterfly, then we let it go. Now it works for Mother Earth."

"Very good." Temasah smiled.

"Sir, may I ask a question?"

"Yes, my son."

"Why do you pray to the sun?"

"I do not pray to the sun. The Great Spirit is an unseen power that lives behind the sun, the moon and stars. I pray to the Great Spirit."

Olo was quiet. *A Great Spirit that lives behind the sun must be very powerful*, Olo thought.

"I will pray to him as you do," Olo said.

"Very good." Temasah smiled again.

Later, after the day's, lesson, Olo prepared to deliver water. Edaw stood still while Olo fitted the leather harness. Olo walked ahead to lead Edaw on the path to the spring. Edaw rested while Olo filled the clay vessels by dipping a big gourd into the spring. When filled, the top of the skin was pulled shut to keep the pot up-right. Then Edaw began pulling the travois up the path to the mound.

When they arrived the workers stopped for a drink of fresh water. "Mound building is very hard work. Each man fills his basket with earth, carries it to the top of the mound and dumps it out. Other men stomp it hard with their feet and smooth it with their hands," the mound builder explained.

On his way home, Olo passed a long narrow clay alley where men were playing a game of chunkey. He watched as one man rolled a disk down the alley and two other men sprang after it, throwing their chunkey poles at it. He could hardly contain his excitement when the man whose pole landed nearest the disk, won the game. Chunkey was Olo's favorite game and he loved to watch.

Today as Olo walked away, everyone grew silent. He noticed Nadac standing nearby. His face was closed, as if guarding a secret, and his nostrils quivered in rage. "Look who's here, the high and mightly one." Nadac pointed to him.

Suddenly, Nadac made a loud, shrill sound. Olo jumped.

"Well, the dummy can hear even if he won't speak. Look at the fire in his cheeks." Nadac doubled over with laughter, pointing his finger and jeering. Then he turned and ran away.

Olo's cheeks burned with embarrassment. As he walked away laughter followed him. *Why is Nadac doing this to me? Is it because I stutter? I find happiness in everything about my new village except these taunts from Nadac. Why does he hate me so much?*

CHAPTER 8

OUTSIDE, THE PLAZA was empty. A cold wind blew and gray wet drizzle forced everyone inside.

Aching bones kept Temasah on his pallet of skins. He raised himself on an elbow. The cornhusk mattress under the skins crackled with each movement.

"Let us review all you have learned. I want to see how you remember my words."

Legs crossed under him, Olo sat and took a deep breath. "A g-good shaman hears with his heart and his ears."

"Good." Temasah smiled with pleasure at the earnest expression on Olo's face.

"Shamans use a wide variety of herbs, roots, and bark to cure illness." Olo concentrated on his stuttering. He felt tension and struggle in his facial muscles around his mouth. He took another deep breath.

"We have the power to restore balance between Earth and people. When people are sick, they are out of balance with nature. We pray to the spirits that control the earth."

"Do we always say our prayers?"

"No, Sir, sometimes we sing or chant prayers," Olo continued. "We sing songs of joy, thanksgiving and lament." Looking away, in a small voice he said, "I like to sing sad songs of lament."

Olo sighed, then went on. "Dry buckwheat seeds or leaves are eaten to relieve stomach aches or headaches."

"Mistletoe berries, ground into a flour and mixed with water, will cure soreness in the eyes, but do not eat the berries."

"Willowbark, stripped from the tree, then boiled with water, made into tea, eases pain." Olo was out of breath.

"How do you take the bark from a tree?" Temasah asked.

"Always take the bark in short vertical strips. If you girdle the bark around the tree, the tree will die."

"Your memory pleases me," Temasah said sitting up. "Now I am going to tell you things you must never repeat." His old face was stern as he leaned forward into Olo's face.

"I give you secrets you must never tell another living person--until you teach your son to become a shaman."

"When I walk into the spirit world, it is revealed to me what is causing the patient's illness. If an object such as a stone or arrowhead has caused pain, I have to remove this object."

Temasah produced a small arrowhead. To Olo's surprise, he put it into his mouth. "I pretend to suck the arrowhead out of the patient. When I take the arrowhead out of my mouth, he believes he is cured."

Olo sat up. "You mean the patient believes the arrowhead is causing the pain and when you suck it out, the pain goes away with the arrowhead?"

"Yes," Temasah said. "The patient must believe in the treatment."

Olo thought for a few minutes, then picked up the old shaman's clapper rattle. "Why do you shake the rattle over the patient's body?"

"The sound is in the wood all the time, waiting to be released. I release it and it gets the attention of the spirits, so they will speak to me."

"And what does the smoke do?" Olo leaned forward.

"Sometimes the smoke contains herbs to be inhaled. But the smoke wafts upward carrying my prayers to the ear of the Great Spirit."

"I understand," Olo said nodding his head.

"You are chosen, Olo, you will become a great shaman." Olo looked into Temasah's old, clouded eyes and smiled.

But, will I learn to be a good shaman? Olo kept his doubts and fears to himself.

CHAPTER 9

ANNAWA APPEARED IN the doorway and beckoned Olo to follow her. As they walked, she leaned close so only Olo could hear. "I want to tell you a secret," she said softly.

"A secret?" Olo asked.

From the folds of her dress she produced a small clay figurine. She placed it in Olo's hand. "This is a special clay object."

"Why is it special?" Olo asked, turning it in his hands.

"Because it will explode when thrown into a fire."

"Explode!" Olo said, his mouth agape. "Mother, why would I want a figurine to explode?"

Annawa smiled. "Let your mind see this. You are speaking to the council. You want to perform an important ceremony. You want them to pay attention to you. So, you place this clay figurine in the fire. Then you raise your arms and implore the Great Spirit to give you a sign, give you a signal that he hears your prayers."

He interrupted. "So, when the clay figurine shatters, they think the Great Spirit has answered my prayer!"

"Exactly." Annawa smiled. "You have a quick mind, Olo. Now let me tell you how to make one."

He listened intently to her instructions. "Search for loess--a fine-grained silt or clay deposited by the wind. Mix in a small amount of water, just enough to form a figurine. When it is dried, you carry it in your medicine bundle. Before you want to use it, wrap it in a piece of wet rawhide, so it becomes very damp."

"You mean let it dry, then re-wet it just before I want to use it?" He was fascinated.

"Yes, the damp figurine must be thrown into a hot fire. The water inside the clay causes it to shatter."

"What a secret you have given me." He smiled and placed the small clay figurine in his carrying pouch.

Inside the potters' workshop, Olo stopped and looked around. He saw clay pots, water vessels, cooking pots, and a shelf full of clay effigy pipe bowls drying in the still air of the room.

He recognized the pipes she had made. "Is this my face?" he asked. He fitted the pipe in his hand.

"Yes." She smiled as she picked up a pipe bowl. "And this is dog. Does it look like Edaw?"

"Oh, yes," Olo said.

The potter's lodge was a busy place. Women and girls were rolling coils of clay. Others were coiling clay into bowls, or smoothing sides of wet pots with a shell. Others were sitting beside a flat stone crushing and grinding shell to temper the clay.

She showed Olo a flat stone. "This is a limestone slab." Picking up a small round stone, she said, "This stone grinds in the center of the slab. Just like corn is ground into flour."

She led him to a pile of broken ancient potshards. She demonstrated how the shards, placed in the depression in the slab were ground with the stone in her hand.

"I mix the spirits of the old pots into the clay of the new pots. I want you to crush these old shards."

"This is fun," Olo said as he pounded away.

When he finished he had a big pot full of finely ground powder ready to be mixed into the new wet clay.

"Good, my son." She showed her approval with a toothless smile. "Now, find Edaw. Go to the woods with the travois and bring back a load of sticks, twigs and branches. Tomorrow we fire our pots."

The rain had stopped and the sun shone brightly as Olo left the lodge.

"Here, Edaw, come," Olo called.

Edaw jumped for joy when Olo called and ran to him wagging his tail.

"Stand still while I harness you." Olo petted him while adjusting the harness. Olo hoisted the hickory poles on his shoulder. Together they walked to the woods.

Edaw stood patiently while Olo inserted the hickory poles into the harness, and piled the platform with branches, limbs, and sticks. When he had a full load, he tied a rope to hold it securely. Then Olo walked ahead on the path, and Edaw followed, pulling the travois. Together they walked back to the village.

CHAPTER 10

INSIDE THE PALLISADE, as they approached the edge of the plaza, Edaw stopped. He cupped forward both ears and sniffed the air as if aware danger was near.

Olo stopped and looked back. The dog's hackles stood erect. A low growl pulsing in Edaw's throat became an angry bark, then a howl.

Nadac stepped from the cover of the trees, ran toward the travois and with all his strength, grabbed the travois hickory poles and overturned the load of wood. This knocked Edaw off his feet. He yelped. Grunting, he struggled to pull out of the harness and free himself.

"Take this, special one!" Nadac shouted in an angry voice. His features were hardened into fierce, ugly lines.

Startled, Olo looked back to see the travois overturned. Edaw was on his back trying to wiggle out of the harness. The hickory poles and the load of brush kept him pinned down.

"Stop! You've gone too far!" Olo shouted.

Nadac darted toward the trees. Olo ran after him, his lungs bursting and his side a mass of pain.

Olo leaped on Nadac's back and slammed him to the ground with an arm locked around his throat. The smaller Nadac, managed to roll over on his back. Olo, sitting on his chest, held onto his ears and pounded his head on the ground.

Every time Nadac moved, Olo pushed down on his ears.

"You evil tease--you want to fight? I'll fight!" Olo felt rage like he had never before felt.

"You taunt me. You hate me. Why? Why are you doing this to me?" Nadac kicked, clawed and screamed in pain as he tried to get away from Olo.

As Olo looked up and saw a crowd of people that had gathered, Nadac saw his chance. He hit Olo on the head with a rock. Stunned, Olo fell to the ground. Nadac punched and kicked him. Olo tried to get up, get away from the blows, but Nadac tackled him.

Together they fell into the load of branches. They were both scratched, gouged, and bleeding. They wrestled on the ground.

The rock had cut over Olo's eyebrow. Blood poured from the wound, covering his eyes so he could not see. Nadac continued hitting him over the head with a limb from the pile of branches. Olo stumbled and fell forward. He put up his hands and tried to ward off the blows coming down on his head.

"Crawl, you worm, crawl!" Nadac shouted.

Just then there was a blur of white fur. In one leap, Edaw was on Nadac, hackles raised, teeth bared and a growl that raised the hair on the back of every onlooker's neck.

The snarling Edaw, bit his hands, tore at his clothing, and finally found Nadac's foot. Edaw held Nadac's foot with his teeth and bit down harder every time Nadac moved. Edaw's white fur was stained with Nadac's blood.

Nadac screamed in pain, but he managed to get up. He raced into the woods with his hands over his ears and his eyes blinded with tears. A cheer went up from the crowd of on-lookers. They laughed and jeered Nadac as he scurried away with Edaw growling and nipping at his heels.

Edaw returned to Olo and started licking his face, trying to rouse him. Finally, Olo sat up stunned and put a hand up to his head, and staggered to his feet. The crowd was dispersing.

Olo caught sight of Annawa, but she lowered her eyes and made no effort to help him. Olo knew he had to stand erect and make it back on his own.

Now is the time to prove I am a man. Olo thought.

Olo righted the travois, fitted Edaw in the harness, and continued walking to the potter's lodge. He held his head high but limped with every step. He wiped his eye with his sleeve as blood from the gash on his head dripped into his eyes.

I can't open my eye--it has swollen shut.

Releasing Edaw from the harness, Olo unloaded the branches onto a waiting pile of brushwood. Tomorrow it would be burned in the open kiln.

Edaw bounded ahead of Olo as he headed toward Temasah's lodge. Inside, Edaw whined and with a half-hearted wag of his tail, sank to the floor with his head between his paws. He let out a sigh.

Temasah noticed the dog's behavior. "What are you trying to tell me, Edaw? Did something bad happen to you? Is this blood on your white fur? What is it?"

CHAPTER 11

OLO ENTERED THE lodge. Temasah's eyes widened. He stepped closer, looking intently at Olo.

Sitting down, Olo hunched his shoulders and turned away. "Your silence stings my ears. Why do you not speak? Are you displeased with me?"

"No, my son," Temasah answered.

He took Olo's face in his hands. Assessing the damage, he called to Annawa, coming through the door flap, "Bring willow bark tea and wet sassafrass leaves for the wounds."

"Your nose is broken, one eye is swollen shut, you have a cut on your forehead, your lip is swollen and you have many scratches and gouges."

Olo sat without complaint while Annawa cleaned the dried blood from his wounds.

"My heart is sick to see you so," she whispered. She set the willow bark tea in front of him. "Drink as much of this as you can."

"Lie down on your pallet," Temasah ordered. Gently he applied the cool, wet sassafrass leaves.

Olo looked into Temasah's eyes. "Are you displeased with me?" Olo munbled out of the side of his mouth.

Temasah opened a small pouch and dropped a few dried sage leaves on the hot stones of the fire pit. He leaned closer to breathe in the smoke that curled up.

"Hear my words and believe them. I do not lie. I have but little to say about your conflict with Nadac. You show courage defending yourself. Nadac has a dark and savage heart."

Temasah looked into the smoke. "Nadac has invisible scars from wounds no one can see. You cannot cut down your enemy because you have a good heart and know not the ways of battle."

He adjusted a pillow under Olo's head. "But we cannot dwell longer on this painful picture."

Olo spoke with a pale and trembling mouth. "You treat me with great kindness. I find happiness in everything here in my new home. You teach me not to raise my hand against anyone. But, why does Nadac taunt me? Is it because I stutter? He is a thorn in my side. For long now I have endured his taunts. But, no more. He will pick up his teeth with broken fingers if ever he teases me again! Why does Nadac taunt me? I am angry because he brings this conflict into my life." A drop of red blood dripped from his swollen lip. Tears welled up in his eyes.

"Nadac is a bully when he thinks you are afraid of him. We know not why Nadac does as he does. Time will reveal the answer to that question."

"Take another sip of tea. Life always shifts from harmony to struggle. Look your problem in the face. Give it a name. Think about the solution to your problem and the Great Spirit will give you the answer."

Urging Olo to close his eyes, Temasah dropped more herb leaves on the hot stones. He shook gourd rattles and sang incantations in a low voice.

The wind blew outside the lodge, rattling the covers over the smoke hole and blowing the heavy deerskin hanging at the door.

Edaw lay quietly, his nose nuzzled under Olo's hand.

Temasah sang a healing song in soft, low tones. As his mind drifted, Olo thought he heard Temasah sing, "Embrace your pain. You will better understand another person's suffering, because you have been weak and in pain."

But as Olo's eyes closed and his breathing became even, he could not be sure.

CHAPTER 12

OLO SLEPT FITFULLY. Next morning, swollen and bruised, he awoke to pain.

Annawa appeared with hot corn meal. "Eat, Olo, you will feel better."

Olo ate every morsel. The food tasted good. His eyes narrowed and his mouth compressed into a tight line.

"What troubles you?" she whispered.

"I hurt. I want to stay in bed," Olo mumbled.

"No, my son, today you hold your head high and pretend yesterday's conflict never happened."

The wind had died down. It was a crisp, autumn day. Many people were gathered at the potter's lodge to help with the open firing on top of the ground.

Everyone looked at Olo's swollen face but no-one smiled. Even the young men averted their eyes. They knew Olo had defended himself against the bully, Nadac, and they respected him for his actions.

"Place straw in those pots," Annawa ordered. She handed him a basket of dried grass.

The clay pots were placed in a small depression on the ground. Larger pots surrounded smaller pots stacked together with dried corn stalks, grasses and twigs piled on top.

Olo put handfulls of dried grass in every pot. "Why am I d-doing this?" he questioned.

"We must warm the pots by burning straw in them before subjecting them to the heat of the fire."

Large pieces of wood were placed in a circle around the pots. Branches and limbs were stacked in a mound over them. Grass, dried cornstalks, limbs and brush radiated out from the center of the pit.

Olo watched the activity. *Are they making a spiral with the limbs and branches*, Olo wondered.

When all was ready, Annawa silenced everyone. She raised her palms and prayed. "Thank you Sacred Mother Earth, for giving us the clay for our pots and the fire with which we harden them."

A young woman started the fire at the outer edge. The circle of brush would burn from the outside to the center, slowly warming the pots.

"A sudden hot fire would cause our clay pots to crack," Annawa said.

Several people tended the fire, pushing the limbs toward the center as they burned. The fire would burn for many hours. They would be at the job all day and into the night--until the fire had consumed all the wood.

Next day, after the pots had cooled, Olo and Annawa searched through the ashes. They found the effigy pipes. Brushing one off, "This pipe with dog's face, I give to you."

"I can smoke tobacco?" Olo smiled so that his teeth showed white against the dark of his face.

"Yes, for ceremonial occasions, you may smoke. We will find a hollow reed to place into the stem end of the pipe."

Annawa felt a smile grow inside her heart when she heard Olo speak. "You are becoming a man, my son, and must take on new ways."

Olo held the pipe in his hand. *Am I becoming a man? But I have so many questions and doubts. Will I become a good man? Will I become a good shaman?*

CHAPTER 13

WINTER'S APPROACH QUICKENED the pace of daily life at the village. Harvested corn ears were stored in elevated corn bins. Beans and dried corn kernels were stored in elm-bark containers or buried in lined granaries. Acorns, ground into meal, were stored in clay pots.

The smell of pemmican being smoked over a hickory fire wafted on the autumn air.

"Do you know how pemmican is made?" Temasah said as they walked toward the woods to search for roots and bark.

"No, Sir," Olo replied.

"Hunters take deer to the squaws, who cut the hide from the aminal for clothing. They cut the venison into strips to be dried. When the venison is dried, it is pounded into meal, mixed with fat, nuts, berries and stuffed into a gut. Then it is twisted into links and smoked over an open fire."

"I only k-know I like to eat it," Olo said, leading the way along the path.

Temasah searched for places where the forest cover had been thinned. There plants that needed sunshine grew. Different plants grew in shaded areas, and even more different plants grew in marsh lands or swamps. Temasah searched for rare plants whose leaves or roots he needed for making medicine. Some were dried and hung from the rafters of his lodge. Some leaves were brewed into a tea and stored in clay pots.

They came to a sassafras tree. "Stop," Temasah said. "Before we take the roots of a tree for medicine, first we walk four times around the tree, praying to its spirit."

Olo watched Temasah walk around the tree talking to it, then crouch, arms dangling, in order to receive the power of the tree.

"Dig here, Olo. We want a root with many branches at the end."

Olo dug with a wood and antler hoe and a smaller digging stick. When he opened a hole around the root, he chopped at it with a chert tipped knife. When it broke free, he placed it in a rawhide bag and slung it over his shoulder.

Temasah hobbled along the path with his walking stick in one hand and Olo's arm to steady him on the other side.

"You need to learn about everything, Olo. Knowledge is power. The more you know, the more powerful person you will be. Always honor Mother Earth and Father River."

He wondered if he would ever be a powerful man like Temasah wanted him to be. Olo kept his doubts to himself.

They saw men on their daily search for firewood, or other men chopping forest deadfall. "An extra store of wood will be a welcome sight on a snowy, winter day." Temasah was in a talkative mood.

The bottomlands along the river were dotted with dense stands of cane.

"Look," Olo shouted as he spied an eagle feather caught in the branches of cane.

"It is a prized feather. You can put it in your sacred medicine bundle." Temasah smiled.

For weeks, Olo had felt paralyzed by sadness, but then his mood shifted. He began to feel good again. His wounds healed, but his face bore permanent reminders of his fight with Nadac. Olo's long nose was no longer straight. A scar marred his forehead disturbing the symmetry of his eyebrow.

"Ah, there is the prickly ash tree I have been looking for." Temasah walked toward the tree.

"Come, Olo. Let me watch you take the bark."

Olo prayed and talked to the tree. "Prickly ash tree, I approach your spirit with great respect. Your bark will be used for good medicine." He used the chert tipped knife to loosen the bark and cut small vertical strips. As he was folding the strips for his pack, Temasah approached. "Do you remember how we use this?"

"We use boneset mixed with prickly ash bark tea for colds and fevers."

"Good, Olo," Temasah said smiling.

As Olo stepped forward, he glanced down and saw a large copper-colored snake, coiled and ready to strike. He jumped back. "Look! A snake!" Olo shouted. He picked up a large rock. "I will kill it," he said.

"No!" Temasah cried. "Snake means you no harm. Like us, he hunts food for survival. He is too small to eat us. Stand very still. He will crawl away."

Together they watched the serpent uncoil and disappear into the reed thicket.

Temasah spoke in a solemn voice. "We live between two worlds, the upper world and the under world. These worlds are opposed to each other. Snakes are messengers from the underground spirits. If you kill snake, you bring trouble and danger into your life."

He raised his arms, his palms to the sky. "Great Spirit, observe. We mean no disrespect for snake. We let him go on his way."

Together they returned to the village. In the lodge, Temasah tired from his outing, lay on his pallet. He watched Olo put the harness on Edaw.

"Your ability to learn pleases me."

"I want to be a good shaman," Olo replied.

"That you will be, my son. Someday spirits will speak to you."

Olo smiled at old Temasah, then he and Edaw set off on their daily task.

At the end of the day, as they were on their way home from delivering water to the mound builders, Olo decided to look for feathers in the cane bottomlands down by the river.

He saw a crowd at the riverbank watching dugout canoe races. He had seen men of the village chop and burn a tree, making a simple boat for fishing or traveling on the water.

As he unhitched Edaw and leaned the travois poles on a tree, his eyes roamed the crowd. He spied several faces he recognized. "Are they having a contest?" he called out.

He saw several boys racing the dugouts, paddling as fast as they could in the flooded river's swift current. Logs and tree limbs floating downstream made the race dangerous.

The dugout slipped over the surface of the water quietly, like a leaf riding high. Suddenly, the dugout bumped into a submerged log spilling the boys into the water. One boy popped up and quickly swam to the river bank. The other boy flailed the water with his hands, bright red blood covering his eyes and forehead.

Olo knew he was watching a dangerous situation. The boy was in peril. Without hesitation, he scrambled down the river bank and dove into the water.

Edaw's loud, excited yelps rang out as he ran back and forth along the river bank.

With strong strokes, Olo swam to the overturned dugout. Several times he dove under water searching for the boy. *Oh, where is he? I only see muddy water*!

He came up, gasping for air. He looked around. Just then he saw a head bob to the surface down stream. With swift strokes he swam to the rescue, grabbing him by the hair and pulling his head above water. Locking one arm around his head, he swam with the other arm toward the river bank.

The crowd had followed them. Loud cheers went up! Many hands pulled the two boys to the safety of dry land. The boy was badly wounded with a bloody gash over his eyebrow. He retched river water he had swallowed and groaned in pain. When rolled over, Olo saw his face.

"Nadac!" he cried.

CHAPTER 14

OLO FORGOT HIS surprise. He chose four strong men. "Arrange the travois to carry a man." They hurried to fasten a robe over the hickory poles. "Take Nadac to Temasah's healing lodge." Olo ordered.

Four men carried the unconscious Nadac up the path, into the village and across the plaza to the small healing lodge next to Temasah's lodge.

The exciting news of Olo's heroic deed spread throughout the village. Everyone greeted him with smiles, handshakes, and words of praise. He was a hero.

Edaw followed closely at Olo's side, his tail between his legs.

Olo's face was stoic but in his mind a storm raged. *Will Nadac hate me even more because I saved his life? Did I shame him?*

Lightning slashed across the sky. Dark clouds appeared overhead and a cold wind blew. *It's as if the Great Spirit makes the weather imitate my mind.* Olo shivered as the cold wind blew against his wet clothing.

He entered the healing lodge. Annawa fanned the flames of a newly lit fire in the central pit. Nadac was laid on a pallet of skins. When the men departed, she removed Nadac's wet clothing, down to his loin-cloth, then covered him with a soft, doeskin blanket.

Temasah entered. He rolled Nadac's limp body over, face down. He rubbed upward on his back until more river water poured from his mouth. From medicine bundles hanging on the walls of the lodge, Temasah chose sassafras leaves and gave them to Annawa to be soaked.

He turned to Olo. "Place tobacco in a pipe and put fire to it, so the sacred smoke can carry my prayers up to the Great Spirit."

Olo filled the pipe, lit it, and handed it to Temasah. "Take this clapper-rattle. Release the sounds and listen to my words."

From a small pouch, Temasah sprinkled herbs on the hot coals in the firepit. Then, with both hands, he held the smoking pipe over his head. The Great Spirit got the first puff. Then he held the tobacco to the east, south, west and north.

He sat cross-legged beside Nadac. Temasah's body twitched. After entering a trance, he began to mumble, "I am a long time traveling. I am entering a silence. My dreams tremble like stones when the winds blow through."

Olo could not understand Temasah's meaning. He saw that Temasah held a black rock in his hand.

"Spirit helper, make my prayer as strong as this rock," Temasah prayed.

Olo could see the imprint where he held it in his hand, almost cutting into his palm.

"Great Spirit above, Nadac's life depends on you. Make him better. Let him live. Let him be healthy. Heal the wound in his heart as well as the wound on his head. His brother awaits."

There was no response in Nadac. It looked as though his spirit had left his body but from time to time, Nadac's eyes rolled from side to side under his closed eyelids.

Olo heard singing. Members of a healing society, summoned by Annawa, sang outside the door. The powerful songs of prayer were sung by members who had visions. The short verses were woven in and out of a chanting melody. A soft drum beat between verses, like a heartbeat.

Nadac's father appeared in the doorway. He watched silently. His eyes never met theirs. His shame was written on his face. He joined the family group gathered there to mourn.

Temasah, in a trance, continued to stare into the other world. In a low voice Olo heard, "Evil walks with you, Nadac. You choose always to do wrong. Black clouds hover over you. Your thoughts are knotted-up. Your heart has turned to ice. You are sour-faced. An evil lives beneath your skin."

Temasah stood up. "Come out! Let this boy go. Why do you make him walk with evil? Out, demon spirits, out!" Temasah shouted.

Olo stood up. He made a line of cornmeal encircling the two. He sat down and started a soft rhythm with the clapper rattle.

" Great Spirit, hear my prayer. Let my words fly to your ear." Temasah chanted in a soft voice.

Then in his normal voice, "Nadac, hear me. You have a choice. You are in a place between life and death. You die and go to the Great Spirit, or you can return to this world. You can return as a different person. You will no longer be a bully. You will no longer walk with evil. You will return as a person capable of love and kindness. You can return as a person with the heart to lead our people."

Temasah softly chanted to the rhythm of Olo's rattle. He urged Olo to join him in the chant. Together they sang.

Slowly, Nadac opened his eyes. "Where am I?"

"You are in Temasah's healing lodge."

"Why did you save me?" Nadac asked, looking at Olo.

"The Great Spirit entered my head and spoke to my heart. A still, small voice said he did not want me to stand by and let the spirit of Father River devour you."

Nadac's brow wrinkled in a frown.

"The Great Spirit told me to save you. He said I am your brother and I am to show you the way," Olo spoke softly.

Nadac looked at Temasah. "Why did you heal me? Am I worth healing?"

"That is a question only you can answer, Nadac." Temasah adjusted the doeskin blanket. He placed damp sassafrass leaves on Nadac's head wound. "We are the choices we make. When we do good, we please the Great Spirit."

Temasah summoned Nadac's family. They agreed to stay with him overnight and care for him. Annawa appeared with willow bark tea for Nadac and a basket of food for the family.

Temasah, Olo, and Annawa came through the door flap to find Edaw wagging his tail, happy to see them. Olo was glad to get into dry clothes and eat supper.

Later that night talking to Temasah, Olo felt uncomfortable. He confided to Temasah, "I surprised myself when I jumped in the river."

"You acted out of love for your fellow man. You are a true hero, my son. Accept the words of praise in your heart."

That night, in the warmth of his bed with Edaw curled up beside him, Olo went over the day's events in his mind. *I feel different somehow. I feel as if the river water washed my mind clean and I left all my worries there in the river.* Olo turned over, gave Edaw a goodnight caress, and closed his eyes.

CHAPTER 15

NEXT MORNING, OLO'S lesson was interrupted. "When the sun is directly overhead, you are to appear before the high chiefs in the main council house atop the great mound," a messenger said.

Annawa lay out Temasah's finest robe, his carved shell gorget, and copper ear spools. She set about combing and braiding his white hair. Age lines etched the corners of his dark eyes, giving his long walnut face an air of dignity.

"How beautiful," Olo exclaimed, when Annawa brought out the tunic and leggins she had made for him. Olo held the butter-soft doeskin in his hands. A lump gathered in his throat. *No one has ever given me such a gift.* His eyes filled with tears. To hide his emotions, he eagerly put on the new clothes.

Annawa combed Olo's hair and arranged a top knot. She inserted the eagle feather.

Annawa stood before him and proudly held a necklace in her hands. "Do you remember when you caught the eagle's prey?"

"Yes, I do,"

"These are the rabbit's teeth. I strung them into a necklace for you." She reached over his head and laid the necklace around his neck. She stood back to admire her work.

"Never in my life has anyone given me such finery." Olo felt hot tears well up in his eyes. "Thank you, Mother," he whispered in her ear.

Olo found his never-used effigy pipe and tucked it in his belt. "Just in case I am invited to smoke."

A chill in the air bit at Olo's face and hands, as they crossed the plaza. Temasah entered the council house and took his seat with the chiefs and elders. Temasah had lived many seasons as a man and used his shamanic skills to ease pain and help cure illness within the tribe. He was a respected member of the elite rulers, and head shaman of the organized priesthood.

Again, Olo was asked to wait outside the house until summoned. *This time I do not have a heavy heart,* he thought. Smoke from cook fires curled into the noon-day sky. Up from the plaza, he heard the rhythmic thumping of pestles being driven into hollow-stump mortars. Women were pounding corn meal into flour for corn bread.

Olo's wait was short. A guard bade him enter and held open the brightly painted door flap. The scent of spiced hickory oil greeted his nose. Smoke from many pipes curled on fragrant clouds that floated through the room.

His eyes adjusted to the dim interior. The firebowls gave off the only light, except for the sun shining through the open smoke hole.

He noticed the men gathered were dressed in their finest clothing. Nadac's father, a minor chief, looked down when their eyes met.

Olo was ushered inside a circle of seated chiefs and elders of the village. Before him, three high chiefs sat on a platform higher than the others. The chief in the center, banged the butt end of his carved wooden staff before he spoke. "Boys achieve manhood by their accomplishments." The chief's deep voice filled the room.

He turned to Olo. "In the time you have lived with us, we have come to know your heart. The magical event with the eagle, foretold your destiny."

Again, he spoke to the room. "Your courageous deed has been noted by this council. Down through the ages, storytellers will recite your story of bravery. How, in the river, you snatched the boy from the jaws of death. How Temasah wrestled with evil spirits and brought him back to life."

The chief's black eyes looked into Olo's. "Your heroic deed proves you are worthy of adoption into our tribe. You will begin preparations for your vision quest. Upon your return, the ceremony for your adoption will be an occasion for festivities. At that time you will receive a bird clan tattoo, and take your new name, Olosah, son of our venerable shaman, Temasah."

The meeting concluded. He banged the staff four times. The members were dismissed.

Olo and a guard helped Temasah down the steps of the mound. Walking to the lodge, Olo wondered if he was misunderstanding something. When they pushed back the heavy door drape and started in, Olo, not wanting the words to be heard, whispered to Temasah, "What is a vision quest?"

Temasah removed his fine clothing. In his old robe he lay on his pallet of skins. Annawa came with an ointment. She sat rubbing his feet.

"Young men seek spirit helpers by means of a vision quest. You will be required to go to a lonely spot. You will then pray to make your heart clean, and to prepare your spirit for messages that come from the spirit world. You will in that lonely place, pray for a personal totem."

"A personal totem?"

"Yes. This totem is the personal protector of its holder. It will forewarn you of danger. It will extricate you from difficulty."

"How will I know my totem when I see it?"

"Your heart will know and tell you." Temasah spoke leaning in to look into Olo's eyes.

"But I am bird clan. The eagle is my totem," Olo protested.

"Son, the eagle is your clan totem. You were born bird clan. You also need a personal totem. It will come to you after a fast and a lonely vigil, far from human habitation."

"Where will I find this lonely place?"

"I will tell you how to find the cave, the home of the underground spirits. I will instruct you how to make your heart clean and how to prepare your spirit for messages that come from the spirit world."

Temasah closed his eyes and began to chant a song of invocation to the unseen powers. "Open my heart to your whisperings," he sang.

"Olo, memorize these words. Repeat them again and again in a chant," Temasah ordered.

Olo chanted the words, "Open my heart to your whisperings, open my heart to your whisperings."

Just then, Annawa dropped Temasah's foot and sat upright. "Olo, you must eat venison from a strong deer. You must not eat meat from rabbit, a shy, anxious animal. Eat only those foods known to come from strong, cunning animals." She massaged one foot.

"And you must eat from the three sisters, corn, beans, and squash." She massaged the other foot.

"I know! You must eat raccoon, a fierce, shrewd animal under attack. Tomorrow I will find raccoon meat for you to eat." She dropped Temasah's foot again. Lost in thought, she walked away, softly mumbling to herself.

CHAPTER 16

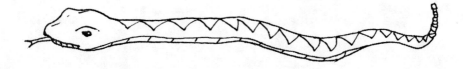

THE NEXT DAY was spent preparing for Olo's vision quest. Annawa scurried around obtaining items, while Temasah tried to warn him of every danger he might encounter.

"Enter the forest on a path of your own choosing. Be careful. Be wary, but make your own path." Temasah spoke urgently as if in a great hurry lest he forget.

"I feel my powers retreating. I must pass them on before the doors in my mind close," he mumbled.

"But, Sir, I f-fear many things. How do I overcome my fears?"

"The first rule is to keep an untroubled spirit. The second is to look your problem in the face and know it for what it is." Temasah shifted his shoulders. He looked into Olo's face.

"What do your fear, Olo?"

"I fear snakes and bats and--"

Temasah interrupted. "Say, snake, I see you. I am afraid of you. But I respect you and will keep my distance from you. I will not impede your path."

Temasah paused. He sat for a moment, his head lowered as if a sad memory had entered his mind. When it had passed, he spoke in a soft voice. "Snakes have a curious way of appearing and disappearing as if my magic. They shed their skins when they grow. They are born anew. They are powerful messengers from the underworld."

"Should we kill them?"

"Never! Snakes bring the rain down from the sky to make our corn grow. Without corn our people will go hungry."

"You mean snakes have powers?"

"Yes, snakes have some secret power that makes the clouds gather and the rain to fall."

Temasah placed two hands on his chest and pulled open his tunic. "Look at the tattoo I proudly wear on my chest."

A black tattoo started in a spiral at Temasah's stomach and curled between his old, sagging breasts. The open mouth of the serpent tattoo ended with a small leather pouch suspended on a cord around Temasah's neck.

"How strange," Olo said.

Temasah removed the pouch, opened it, and emptied into Olo's hand, a perfect, round pearl. He held it in his palm, then turned it with his fingers. "What is this? It looks like the beautiful, full moon."

"Great Spirit causes the mussel laboring in the river bottom mud to create a thing of beauty."

"In the river?"

"Yes. I wear this pearl to honor the snake that swallows the moon. It was given to me by my great and wise mentor. When I am gone home to the Great Spirit, you will return this precious thing to its rightful place and dedicate it in my honor."

Olo's eyes filled with tears at the thought of Temasah's death. He wanted to change the subject.

"And b-bats?"

"Creatures of the night are there because the Great Spirit makes it so. They serve Mother Earth. Their work is in the night. You need not fear them. Just keep your distance."

"But, h-how will I know the right choices to make?"

"You are intelligent, level-headed, and resourceful. Think about what you plan to do. You are responsible for your actions. Consider all the consequences of your actions. The Great Spirit lives in every living thing, in trees, in birds, in animals. Pray to him. He will watch over you and guide you to the right choices."

"Yes, I suppose you're right." Olo frowned. He wanted to express his fear of the future, but he could not find the words.

Annawa entered with a steaming pot of raccoon stew and a basket of corn cakes. "The raccoon meat will make you strong," she said. "Eat."

"My Mother saves tender morsels for me," Olo said. He ate the stew, corn cakes, and hickory nut butter she had prepared. "Your cheeks are no longer pinched," she whispered.

"For your quest, I have pemmican." She held up lengths of the delicacy. "And a gourd water bottle, should you be unable to find fresh water."

Temasah leaned back with a cup of pine needle tea in his hand. "Remember to turn to your right in the cave. The rocks you want are very old. They remember when Earth was young."

He gazed intently into Olo's eyes. "All those rocks have voices but not everybody can hear them. You have to listen very carefully. Dedicate your spirit to them."

Annawa reappeared. "May I interrupt? I have set out items you may need on your quest."

Olo and Temasah followed her. Olo saw a leather back pouch stuffed with a warm pelt blanket. A length of rope lay neatly coiled beside it. A quiver full of arrows lay under a long bow. A hardwood club and a chert knife with a staghorn handle lay with it.

Olo looked at Annawa. "You may need to protect yourself. There are bears in the forest." She had a worried look on her face. Apologetically she held up a basket of corn cakes and links of smoked pemmican.

Temasah stepped forward. With the tip of his cane he pointed to the items Olo would need. The back pouch with the warm blanket, the rope, the chert knife and the pemmican.

"Fetch the leggins and moccasins," he ordered. He reached out to Olo. "This soft piece of leather you will need at the cave entrance." He placed the piece in Olo's hands.

"In the cave, why?"

"You will understand when the time comes," Temasah confided. Then he turned and walked away. "We must retire early. Tomorrow at dawn you begin your quest."

CHAPTER 17

NEXT MORNING DAYBREAK found Olo dressed in his long tunic, leggins, and moccasins. He sheathed the chert knife and secured it to his belt. He tied the pemmican around his waist. *Just like father had tied the bundle of effigy pipes around his waist.* Olo had a brief picture of his father in his mind.

Edaw sensed the excitement and pranced around. "You can not go with me. You must stay here." Olo petted his soft white fur. His words fell on deaf ears. Edaw continued to jump around in anticipation.

Temasah entered the lodge, returning from his daily prayer to the rising sun. "Keep this safe and dry, my son. You will need it at the cave."

He placed a piece of red ochre in a little leather bag in Olo's hand. "First carve the spiral intaglio deep into the surface of the stone cave wall. Then trace the red ochre in the groove you have made. Make your spiral beside the one I made many years ago. Make it beside the one my father made before me."

"And then I p-pray to the underground spirits and ask their blessings. I dedicate my life as a shaman to them."

"Yes, my son, you remember your lessons well." Temasah's old face was solemn.

"Your vision quest will be seven sleeps of isolation to face your fears, find your spirit voice, and your personal totem. My heart grows heavy when I think of the dangers you face. But I have confidence in your ability to see trouble and avoid it."

Annawa entered. She walked slowly with downcast eyes. Her sad, tear stained, walnut face was wet with tears. She sat down with a faraway look in her eyes. "In sleep the body rests. Dreams are important. A person's dreams tell what his soul needs to remain strong. Only if the soul gets what it desires will a person have good fortune in life."

Temasah gently laid his hand on her head and in a soft voice asked, "What ails you?"

"I slept badly last night. Faint and far away I heard the screech of an owl, a bad omen, a portent of danger. Something bad is coming. Be careful, Olo, danger walks with you."

With tenderness, Olo embraced her. "I will be careful. I will return to you, Mother." Olo's heart beat in his throat.

Temasah raised his hands. "Oh, Great Spirit, make Olo one with the spirits. Give him the strength to endure all they give him to bear." His old, wrinkled face looked sad.

Temasah leaned to look in Olo's face. "You are first in my eyes and first in my heart," Temasah whispered.

Olo felt a lump in his throat and pushed back tears as he embraced the old man. He gathered up his back pouch, slung the rope over his head and shoulder, and went out the door.

Edaw pawed the ground. He whined and backed up. Suddenly, he bolted out the door and bounded up beside Olo. "No, Edaw, stay!"

Edaw stopped. He stood on stiff legs and stared at Olo with large wondering eyes. He turned his head from side to side in bewilderment, then jumped up and ran ahead of Olo. "No, Edaw!" Olo ran to catch him. He picked him up and carried him back to the lodge, all the while the wriggling Edaw covered his face and neck with wet kisses.

Temasah stood at the door with a piece of rope to tie Edaw inside the lodge. Olo hurriedly walked away from the lodge. Edaw's hurt cries of disappointment rang in his ears. His pain tore at Olo's heart. He could still hear Edaw's howls as he walked out the pallisade gate.

Under a sad, gray sky, a cold wind blew. Olo walked across a corn field. His heavy moccasins protected him from the sharp stubble. Olo stopped on a rise and took one last look back at the mounds and the village nestled in the crook of the river. He listened to the sounds. A hawk shrilled above and in the distance the sound of a dog barking--was it Edaw?

"I know my old village lies to the north and east of here, but my desire to return is lacking. This is my home." Olo took courage from the sound of his voice.

He walked toward the woods. "I know spirits live in the forest and it is wise to establish one's identity before entering." He called, then waited. He got no response. He chose to enter the forest at a place that looked promising. The stillness of the forest was interrupted by the shrill cry of a bluejay. Deer broused through the willows and sycamores. The sky filled with swirling flocks of birds. Turkeys clucked and ratcheted, and grouse made an eerie drumming that Olo felt more than heard.

He passed women gathering chestnuts. They took no notice of him. Down by the river men gathered hemp. They did not hear him. "Rope, mats, trump lines, and baskets are made from hemp." He counted on his fingers.

Thick fog hung over the river as he walked along. Ducks spread over the waters, paddled and dived Cranes stalked small creatures in the shallows among the reeds. Birds of prey soared silently overhead looking for food. High in the sky, large flights of geese flying south, appeared in the sky.

All day he walked with strong, confident steps. Late in the day he came to a bluff overlooking the river. From there he could see across a series of timbered ridges that turned from pale gray to deepest gray in the distance. Along the western horizon thunderheads were piling up and lightning shot across the blackest of the storm clouds. The wind shifted and became colder.

"I should make camp here before the storm comes." He felt good hearing the sound of his own voice.

He set about making a lean-to with branches and boughs. He was just finishing when a roll of thunder caught his attention and the sky darkened abruptly. Close around him everything turned still. Birds fell silent. A burst of wind swept across the sky bringing chill rain.

He snuggled back into the farthest corner of the shelter with his head resting on his leather pouch and his pelt blanket turned fur side in. Soon he was fast asleep.

CHAPTER 18

ONCE DURING THE night, the distant howling of wolves broke the silence. Olo awoke and reached for a big stick. He felt to make sure his knife was still in its sheath tied to his belt. Reassured, he fell back to sleep.

The brightness of the sun blinded him and made his eyeballs ache. Olo sat up and rubbed his eyes. Then he held his hands up and prayed the morning prayer as best he could remember it.

He walked and kept sight of the river to his left. "Poor Edaw," Olo said between bites of pemmican. "He was disappointed. But today I must make good time. I want to find the trail to the cave before sundown." He doubled his pace.

At noon that day he came to a spot in the river where waters widened and darkened, extending into reed beds and swamps that smelled of mud and decaying vegetation.

"I should cut some reeds for torches," he said. He took out the chert knife and hacked at the reed stems. When he had a large pile, he rolled the reeds into a bundle and tied them with a dried vine.

"Now I can dispell the darkness of the cave with light from the burning torches." He felt very proud and confident as he hoisted them on his back.

By mid-afternoon, he was surprised to see rapids running in the river. By the time he reached the falls, he suspected that he might have passed the trail to the cave.

A black turkey buzzard glided in circles just above him, dropping lower and lower. He could see its reddish eyes fixed on him. "Shoo. . . go away!"

The river ran narrow past a low cliff. He spotted the faint trail that twisted, growing narrower as it seemed to climb to the sky . On the hill in the distance, lay the forest.

"This is a hard climb through brush and deadfal." He panted as he made his way through the woods.

He approached a large rock outcrop. He stopped as if frozen in mid-step. A thrill of fear ran up his spine. There before him lay many snakes. He watched them curl and slither on top of each other as they crawled into the hole in the rocks. One by one they slithered down into the hole and disappeared.

Olo felt his hands tremble with fear. A cold wind blew his tunic and he shivered. "Cold weather will soon be upon us. At this time, snake is going into his hole to sleep through the winter." He spoke softly to himself for fear the snakes would hear him.

He remembered Temasah's words. "Do not impede his path. Say, snake, I see you. I fear you. You have my respect. Go on your way." He spoke the words under his breath and made a big circle around the snake rock.

On the other side of the rock outcrop, he again found himself in deep woods. He had walked for some time. He heard movement and turned to see a bear. Again he froze in his tracks.

He heard Temasah's words in his memory, *It is bad luck to disturb a bear that has a young one at her side.* He could not see if she had a cub with her or if she was alone.

"I must be downwind of her. She too is looking for a winter sleep hole in the rocks," he whispered to himself. The bear slowly lumbered away in the other direction.

He stood and looked around. He saw the trail dip into a copse of oaks tangled with brush, then rise again, emerging along a slope dotted with brush. It seemed to end at the base of a limestone bluff.

Olo clasped both hands over his mouth. He mumbled into his hands. "There it is! The entrance to the cave lies straight ahead. That black hole in the cliff is the entrance to the cave!"

He walked quickly, intent on getting up the slope. He wanted to find a good spot to make camp before nightfall.

At the base of the bluff, he found a log, recently downed by a windstorm, and used it as a place for his camp. He gathered brush, saplings and boughs to make a lean-to against the fallen log.

It was late afternoon. He gathered sticks and started a fire. He added wood shavings very slowly. When the fire burned brightly he pulled a downed sapling and added it to the fire. It crackled and burned. Soon twilight darkened the sky.

He drank some of the water and ate pemmican. He sat looking into the coals and tried to remember everything Temasah had said. "Not all spirits are good. Some seek to harm us. Never forget to honor good spirits. Keep them on your side so they will not abandon you to the power of the evil spirits."

"Tomorrow I make my heart clean and prepare my spirit for messages. Tomorrow I enter the cave."

CHAPTER 19

AT DAWN THE next morning he sat naked and greeted the rising sun with the morning prayer. Then he prayed his personal prayer.

"Great Spirit, look down and see me seated in front of my holy home, the cave. I come to pay homage to the underground spirits and to carve my spiral intaglio next to my father's spiral. Hear my prayers. Guide my footsteps. Let my ears hear your messages, my mind understand, and give my body the strength to obey them."

He dressed. He took out the small piece of doeskin Temasah had given him and tied it securely onto his belt under the chert knife and next to the little bag that held the piece of red ocher.

He stashed his pack pouch, extra reeds, fur blanket, rope and pemmican under the log lean-to.

"This is a safe place. Besides, I will return this afternoon. My vision will come quickly."

He walked to the bluff and climbed up the boulders. The mouth of the cave was up the hillside- -an opening shaped like a scar. Half way he stopped to rest, and realized his mind was full of questions.

"Is this cave full of snakes or bats? I am afraid of both. Can snakes climb up this high?" Olo talked to himself.

He climbed onto the biggest boulder nearest the dark, jagged slit in the rock. There he placed wood shavings in a small depression in the rock. He knelt down, briskly rubbed a stick between his hands, then fanned and blew the sparks until he coaxed a feeble flame out of them. Then he put some tiny twigs on and fanned them to life. When the flames rose he put light to the reed torch.

Holding the torch in front of him, he wriggled through the narrow entrance to the cave. When he stood up, he found himself enveloped in an odor so strong it was overpowering. His eyes, nose and throat burned. He coughed and gaged. He wanted to vomit. He dropped the torch.

Holding his nose, he scrambled back through the slit in the rock. He took a deep breath of fresh air. "Temasah knew about this horrible odor. That is the reason for the soft doeskin! I am to wear it over my face!"

Olo inhaled several more times, then tied the skin over his mouth and nose. Wriggling back through the rock opening. He found the torch. Part of it still burned. He knocked off the ends of the reeds so they all burst back into flame.

The light from the reed torch gave off light suddenly revealing for an instant the walls and vaulted ceiling of the cavern. The torch light made eerie shadows on the walls. There clinging to the cave ceiling, were masses of bats! Big bats and little bats rustled and shifted position overhead. All of them squirming, making soft squeaking, grunting noises, and raining down urine from their little bladders.

They all flew in confusion and turmoil, then they settled back in new positions.

"I disturbed their tranquility and frightened them into urinating," Olo instinctively understood.

The terrible smell made him hold his nose. His mouth was agape under the doeskin. He looked down at the floor of the cave. It was covered with bat guano with living worms and beetles crawling in the droppings. An infant bat had fallen into the thick guano and was being eaten alive by the big beetles. He watched its pitiful efforts to get away from the beetles.

"Did my torch cause the baby to let go of its mother?" Olo felt a stab of guilt as he watched the new born bat give up its spirit and lie still in death.

"I've got to get out of here!"

Holding the torch with one hand and his nose and mouth with the other, he hurried to the back of the cave.

It was an unpleasant cave--a cramped, slanting hole in the rock, where he had to stoop and sometimes crawl on his belly in order to get around. The cave, cool and dark, smelled of dust and was so quiet that his whispers echoed from the dome of its ceiling, where in some of the deep cracks bats clung.

He crawled and wiggled in a prone position through passage ways before he could stand upright. He made his way through a narrow, winding corridor. The air lost the terrible bat guano stench. Cool, fresh air calmed his fears. He tore off the doeskin mask covering his face. He leaned against the cave wall to catch his breath.

"I must stay calm. I can breathe now. The bats do not live in this part of the cave." The sound of his own voice reassured him.

The way was difficult--full of twists, turns, climbs and crawls, and dead-end passages. He came out into an open space. His torch lighted a vast cavern where he saw a frozen waterfall glistening like moonlight on snow. "I've never seen anything like this! What a beautiful sight."

In wonder and awe, he turned the light from the reed torch to reveal the interior of the cave. He saw delicate wet stone that dripped down from the ceiling of the cave to almost touch the deposite of stone that seemed to grow up from the cave floor.

"It's like fingers almost touching." He was astonished by the sight of the stone formation. "This cave is a strange and beautiful place. The tears of underground spirits hang like ice in the wintertime."

He found another corridor to the right that descended to a lower level. He came upon another sight. "Wavy lines, zig-zag lines, square shaped signs, dots. . . what do they mean? Is this a sign I should know?" He tried to remember if Temasah had ever talked about a message on the cave walls?

Farther along he saw ancient torch smudges on the cave walls beside hand prints. "I see places where people have rubbed smoldering torches against the walls, removing the ash so they would flare anew. I know ancient people have been here. Maybe they were here on a vision quest just as I am now."

The passage again opened on a vast cavern. He kept his eyes down and stepped carefully. He was walking on a narrow ledge with the cave wall on one side and a black drop-off on the other. The path went over a narrow lip of rock. He heard several rocks slide off and drop. Then he heard a splash.

"Water fills the bottom of this cavern." He slowed his pace and stepped even more carefully. A shiver of fear ran up his spine. "I must remember to put my weight nearest the wall."

The ledge flattened to solid rock. Then he saw it. "There is the ancient spiral! It looks like the sun! Long ago, someone pecked spirals, a moon, and a hand. The designs on the rocks are strange. Temasah said they would be on the right side."

He held the reed bundle close to the cave wall so he could judge which spiral seemed to be the youngest. With the chunk of red ocher clay, he marked a spiral of his own.

"My knife will do a better job," Olo talked to himself as he scraped away at the stone.

He looked down. "I see where someone dropped a broken blade." He picked it up and finished carving the spiral with it. "Now I trace the intaglio with red ocher until it is a bright, new spiral on the cave wall."

He sat cross legged on the floor of the cave, with his hands raised, palms up. "Oh, Great Spirit, hear my prayer. This spiral I carve in homage to the underground spirits, just as my father, Temasah did, and his father before him. Look down and see that my head is clear and my heart is pure. I dedicate my life to good works."

CHAPTER 20

HE SAW THAT his cane reed torch was burning low. "I must go while I can still see the way." He picked it up, turned and hurried off.

He scrambled along the ledge. Suddenly, the rock collapsed under his feet! He found himself falling through air. In the inky blackness, he heard screams. He realized they were his own.

His body plunged into the water, then popped up to the surface. He gasped in a deep breath. He swam furiously in darkness. He could not see where he was swimming. Soon, his hand slammed into solid rock. After a moment of confusion, he hoisted himself up out of the water.

He sat there gasping for air. Terror gripped him! He felt like he could not breathe! He heard his heart pounding in his ears. The realization that he was alone in the dark, deep inside the cave, gripped his heart with cold, icy fear. He screamed in panic! He wanted to run around but knew he must sit still in the dark or he would again fall into the cold water. He realized he was trapped.

"Help! Help! Someone help me! Help!" He uttered a garbled scream that ended in a wrenching sob. He screamed again and again in desperation. The sounds echoed in the blackness.

Exhausted, he lowered his head and sobbed. Tears rolled down his cheeks. Despair settled like a rock in the pit of his stomach. Fatigue lay upon him like his sodden clothing. He curled up in a position trying to get warm. He sobbed until he fell asleep.

He woke abruptly and sat up. "Calm... I must stay calm. I am in trouble but I must stay calm."

He realized an intense pain in his ankle and leg. Feeling along his leg, he determined he had sprained it in the fall.

With his hands outstretched, he felt the rock he sat upon. Then he lay down and felt all around to estimate the size of the rock ledge.

"I can safely lie here." The words comforted Olo.

Cautiously, he stood up, then he raised his arms. "I am in an open space where I can stand up. But if I step, I may step into the water. I wish I could see! This blackness is horrible! I hate this blackness!"

Between shivers his teeth chattered, "I am wet and cold." The pain in his leg caused him to sit down.

He pulled off his tunic and leggins and wrung the water out of them. "If I wave them in the air, they will dry more quickly." His voice trembled with cold and fright, and his teeth chattered.

Vigorously he rubbed his skin trying to rub warmth into it. "Maybe if I move my arms and legs they will warm up." But every movement made his leg hurt.

"I have this feeling of hanging in space. I am utterly alone and I only have my voice. The cave knows neither day nor night, only blackness. Great Spirit look down and see me!"

The hopelessness of the situation overwhelmed Olo and he sobbed again. He realized he was hungry also. At length, he fell asleep and slept fitfully, waking in terror many times.

This time when he awoke, he was calm, but he was angry. "Why did this happen to me? Did I not pray all the prayers? Did I not observe all the instructions and do every thing I was told to do? Why has this terrible fate befallen me? What did I do to deserve this? Why did you let this happen to me?"

He howled his rage like a wounded animal. A jagged scream erupted from him. He screamed. He shouted. He did not know who he was angry with, but he cursed the darkness and let his anger out. This was better than the cold, dark silence of the cave where there was no light, no movement, nothing but blackness.

He had feelings he had never felt before--feelings he could not explain. "The rage I feel leaves me sick and weak. Only my voice cuts through this darkness and echoes back to me. Will I go out of my mind with fear?" Olo's thoughts rambled.

"I see a memory. I remember Temasah saying I will find the answer to difficulties in the realm of spirit. Did I offend the underground spirits? Does Mother Earth intend to keep me in her grasp? Am I to die an icy death, alone in the dark? I am afraid to meet the Great Spirit. I do not want to die."

Then he had a realization. "This is a test to build my inner strength. Being cold, wet, hungry and trapped in the darkness is all part of this test." Olo's words ecoed in the stillness. He tried to feel good about his new thought.

"I must learn to develop my other senses. I will hold out. I believe I will pass this test. I will hold out. This must be endured." His voice echoed in the darkness.

"The death of the infant bat was a sign, a warning. I did not see it. I did not understand." Olo's thoughts wandered. Olo rubbed his cold, numb feet.

He began to hum and then to sing the song of lament for the dead. "Singing tells the underground spirits I am alive." He swayed his body from side to side.

"Spirits of the cave, hear me. I am cold and hungry. All is blackness. How do I endure this? Open my heart to your whisperings." Olo again sang the song of lament in low moaning tones. An old memory of his mother's death gave him the words and tempo.

Time went by. Olo did not know whether it was day or night. He shivered and he hungered and he slept. Once, as he was falling asleep, he saw Annawa's face. He tried to recall his young mother's face, but he could not. He did not know how long he had been there in the cave. He knew only the darkness.

Once, he thought he heard Edaw barking. But it was a dream. He rolled over and pretended to put his arms around Edaw's warm, furry body. When the light appeared, he thought he was dreaming. But then a voice called. He sat up.

"This is no dream! This is real! Here! I'm here! I'm here!"

CHAPTER 21

THE LIGHT GOT brighter and brighter. The torch lit up the cavern ceiling, walls and shined on the water. He could see a figure standing on the ledge.

"Nadac! Why are you here? Are you real? Are you part of this test? Have you come here with some dark purpose?"

"No, I have come to save you." Nadac shouted. "I have secured the other end of this rope to a rock formation. I will throw you the rope," Nadac shouted. His words echoed .

Nadac threw the rope but it landed in the water. He held his torch over the ledge. Its brightness illuminated the water.

Olo jumped into the water and swam to the rope. He tied it around his chest under his arms because he felt suddenly tired and his musches felt weak.

Nadac pulled Olo to safety. Together they rushed out of the cave. As they passed through the bat droppings, Olo reached down and picked up the infant bat skull. He paused for a moment. Lifting his eyes toward the ceiling, "Mother bat, forgive me for killing your infant. For my medicine bundle," he said to Nadac. "This is my personal totem for my medicine bundle."

Olo stopped just outside the entrance to the cave. Resting against the rocks, he took a deep breath of fresh air. Under a gray sky a chill wind blew.

Looking down on the camp site, he saw Edaw tied to a tree. Edaw cocked his ears and growled and began wildly yelping, barking, and jumping around.

He tried to hurry down the rocky slope, but his cold, weak muscles trembled and he staggered to his knees. He felt Nadac's arm around his waist and his arm around his shoulders. Slowly they made their way back to the camp.

Nadac had enlarged and reinforced the lean-to with more saplings and boughs. While Olo and Edaw were greeting each other, Nadac lay out the blanket fur side up. He helped peal off Olo's sodden clothing. He rubbed Olo's skin dry with clumps of deer moss.

Olo lay wrapped in the fur blanket with one arm around Edaw. He fell into an exhausted sleep. When he awoke, it was dark. Nadac was tending several large pieces of venison roasting over a big camp fire.

Olo held his hands out to its warmth. "I have not eaten for many days," Olo said in a trembling voice.

Nadac handed Olo his dry tunic and leggings. "I killed a young deer. I saved the liver for you. You are weak from your long stay in the cave. You need food." Nadac handed the liver to Olo.

Hungrily, Olo ate a few bites then lay back. Nadac started to speak, but Olo interrupted. He spoke in a quavering voice. "Nadac, you gave me back my life." Olo sobbed between shivers. Tears rolled down his cheeks.

"I was caught in the bowels of Mother Earth and I thought I would die there. I prayed the Great Spirit would see me. He sent you to find me."

Edaw licked the salty tears from Olo's face, and moved closer to him.

Nadac spoke quickly. "Temasah found me. He looked at me with those milky eyes and said he saw in a vision that you needed me. He said you were in grave danger, and to follow Edaw. Temasah said the underground spirits love you and want to keep you with them. He gave me Edaw to sniff out the trail, a coil of rope, links of pemmican, and this magic talisman."

Nadac held out from his throat, a smooth, shell gorget Olo had seen many times.

"Edaw picked up your scent and we found this camp site in two days."

Olo dried his tears. "I am happy you found me." Olo hugged Edaw's neck and scratched his ears. Edaw licked Olo's face and ears and sat even closer to him.

Together, the three of them ate their fill. That night they slept, snug in the lean-to, while a big log fueled the camp fire through the night.

Next morning, a strong wind wove its way through the branches overhead and a faint, cold drizzle fell. Nadac found a branched sappling and whittled it for Olo to use as a crutch. With sticks and rope, he made a splint to immobilize his ankle. Then he cut off a piece of the fur blanket, wrapped it around his swollen ankle and fitted the splint over it.

"I sprained it when the rock ledge collapsed and threw me into the water." Remembering made a shiver of fear run up his spine.

They spent the day resting and eating venison. Olo felt his strength returning.

"You are a different person, Nadac. What made you change?"

"When you saved me from drowning in the river, I came back to earth as a different person. I got the idea you are my brother. Did I dream that?" Nadac's forehead wrinkled in a frown.

"Temasah has dreams that foretell events to come. Some dreams disturb him, some warn him. In a dream, he saw us as brothers. I am happy you are my brother."

Olo looked into the fire. "Why did you hate me?"

Nadac held his head down. "You are so tall. You are lucky about the eagle's food and the omen. I wanted all that to happen to me. My older brothers are tall, while I am short. They urge me to be bold, then laugh when I am in trouble. Sometimes they tickle me until I soil my pants or loose my water, then laugh at me and call me baby." Nadac looked down at his feet.

"A spirit inside me took over. . . I was angry. . . I do not know why." Nadac raised his head and looked into Olo's eyes. "You are transformed now. You no longer stutter."

"Yes, the vision quest taught me many things. And I will be glad to go away from the cave, and this hidden kingdom of bats."

"I know how you feel. I feared the close quarters of the cave. When darkness enclosed me, I felt I could not get my breath. Tell me, Olo, what vision did you see?"

"I saw no vision. I saw only darkness. But my mind realized I am more than the body I carry around. I am a person inside and I am capable of many things. I lean on the Great Spirit. I look inside for all answers."

CHAPTER 22

BY NIGHTFALL GRAY clouds filled the sky. The night grew colder. The light rain turned to sleet, and the sleet turned to snow. By morning, an early snow muted the valley. All was still.

"It is time to be in the warmth of a lodge," Olo said as he struggled to his feet. "Let's go back to the village."

They shuffled through ankle-deep snow. Edaw, exhilarated by the chill air, raced ahead then turned to stare back at them.

Several times the crutch slipped and Olo fell. He picked himself up. "I can not walk fast."

In the woods snow hung in the trees in large clumps molded into odd shapes by the wind and sun at midday.

Olo and Nadac clambered down a still snowy trail startling a deer. Edaw chased it for a few minutes then pranced back to them. He was in high spirits, playing in the snow.

When they came to the river, there was a thin crust of ice frozen along the riverbank.

"We are making slow time because of me." Olo hobbled faster.

"You are doing your best. You can not do more." Nadac placed Olo's arm over his shoulders and put his arm around Olo's waist.

"I respect your ability to survive an underworld without light and inhabited with strange creatures." Nadac enjoyed talking about the experience they had shared.

Nadac was short in stature with a small compact body. He walked with his head high and his chest out trying to appear taller. His shoulders fit under Olo's straight outstretched arm.

"Yes, I survived my quest but now I am weak, injured and slow."

"But we are on our way back to the village," Nadac said, in a calm voice, trying to change his mood.

"Temasah taught me there is an underworld symbolizing disorder and chaos that exists beneath the earth. Now, I believe him. I have seen it."

They trudged on, slipping and sliding through the snow. Finally, Olo stopped. "My ankle hurts and I am cold. I can not go on." He found a fallen log and slumped down. Edaw sat at his feet.

"I know a way to warm your bones," Nadac said, a trace of a smile curling his lips.

"Rest here while I look for a white oak tree," he shouted as he disappeared into the woods. Soon he returned with an armload of bark. He piled them on the ground.

"Do you know this bark gives a lot of heat from a small amount of fuel?"

"No, I know nothing about this. What are you doing-- digging a hole?"

"Yes, this hole is about the size of my head," Nadac dug in the ground with his chert knife.

When the hole was the right size, Nadac criss-crossed narrow strips of bark until it was filled. Then he tossed his blanket over his head so the wind could not blow out the sparks, and made fire.

He fanned and blew. Soon it was smoldering. "Now, when the bark strips are burning, I will cover the hole with earth, leaving two small holes for draught." Nadac was excited about his project.

"But how can that keep us warm?"

"You will sit with your ankles crossed. This hole is in the space between your knees. With the blanket you cover your head and whole body with just your face out so you can breathe. The heat is captured and it keeps your body warm."

"How will you stay warm?"

"I will make one for myself as soon as this fire glows," Nadac said confidently.

"You must teach me all you know about the ways of the woods, I want to learn," Olo said. Nadac smiled to himself.

As darkness overcame them, they sat hunched over their fires, eating pemmican. There they spend the night, sleeping fitfully.

Next morning they had just started toward the village, when they encountered a hunting party from their village returning with fresh killed venison slung over their shoulders.

They recognized Olo and Nadac immediately, for they had heard the story told around the lodge fires at night. Happy to see them both alive and become part of the story, the biggest hunter carried Olo on his back the rest of the way to the village.

CHAPTER 23

OLO SAW THE familiar path that followed the bend of the river. He got his first glimpse of the village. The flat-topped earthen mound rose higher than the other mounds. "It is good to see the mounds again."

Already he smelled wood smoke. It wasn't long before he could hear faint sounds from the village: dogs barking, people talking, and the playful cries of children.

The trader's heavy dug-out canoes lined the riverbank. "I had forgotten about the festival," Olo said to the man carrying him on his back.

"We are bringing meat for the feast. There will be games, music, and dancing. Everyone is excited about the celebration," he said.

When Edaw found himself on home ground, he bounded ahead, barking with excitement at everyone he met, as if announcing their arrival.

By the time they passed the gate in the pallisade and entered the village, crowds of people lined the way. Olo saw Nadac's father. He did not approach but smiled his approval at the procession and his son's position as rescuer.

Bright sunshine had melted the snow to slush. The broad, open plaza was filled with traders and their bearers who were paid to carry a trader's supply of stone for making tools. Potters put out their wares for anyone who wanted to trade with them. Craftsmen were preparing to lay out their goods for sale or barter. There would be lively trade with many people attending the festival.

The hunter carried Olo to the shaman's healing lodge. "Thank you for your service. I am in your debt."

He placed him on a pallet of skins. A comforting fire glowed under the smokehole and warmed the lodge. Edaw nosed his way past the men and lay down.

Temasah entered the lodge. He scattered corn meal in a circle around Olo, then raised his hands, palms up. "Great Spirit, hear my prayer. I am grateful you chose to return my son, Olo. Bless him and bless Nadac, the rescuer."

He placed his hand on Olo's forehead. "My old eyes behold a wonderous sight: you alive and well." Temasah spoke softly in his ear.

Annawa entered and stood quietly in the shadows, proud, silent tears glistening in her eyes.

Olo could hardly control his voice. "Oh, Sir, I found myself in a cruel situation. I was trapped in the darkness of the cave and...." Great sobs shook Olo's body. "I thought I would die there.... I tried to be brave... but I was afraid...."

Olo could see the concern on Edaw's face as he nudged closer. He pulled Edaw close and stroked his head. "I am so glad to be home." Edaw wagged his tail in response.

"Lie still while I examine your ankle," Temasah said. Annawa was at his elbow, ready to assist him.

"Nadac did a good job with the splint," Temasah said rewraping the wooden stick splint around his ankle. "Elevate this leg with bundles of skins," he ordered.

Annawa brought bundles and placed them under his leg. She leaned down to kiss his face. "My heart is full of joy to have you home," she whispered.

"Mother, I am hungry. Do you have corn cakes and hickory nut butter?" he whispered.

"Yes!" She smiled and hurried through the door flap.

The remainder of the day was spent in discussion with Temasah. "I want to hear about everything you saw, heard, and felt. I am eager to hear about every aspect of your adventure. Do not leave anything out."

For hours, words poured from Olo's mouth. He spoke clearly and distinctly. He did not stutter or hesitate. He related each experience with enthusiasm.

"I am pleased with you. You have been tested. You looked inside yourself and found strength to survive your ordeal. This quest has given you the confidence needed to stutter less."

Olo smiled and listened intently to Temasah.

"When you are an old man, you will remember your vision quest and take strength from it," he said.

Olo pulled the infant bat skull out of his ochre pouch. "My personal totem is a bat." Then he related the incidents in the cave entrance.

"When I see a furry, night creature with long finger-wings, I will always be reminded that I will not give up, I will keep trying."

He held up the tiny, white skull. "This goes into my medicine bundle."

"Bring the thing we have been working on," Temasah said to Annawa.

She fetched a folded bundle and handed it to Temasah. "This new buckskin, prepared by Annawa, will be your medicine bundle."

Temasah spread out a small, oval skin with its edge turned under and sewn into a casing, so an inserted cord could gather it into a bundle.

Olo watched as he flattened it out. On the back was a carefully drawn chart. "Is that a map? Am I going on another trek?" he asked in an urgent voice.

"No, my son, this is a map of the heavens. Your next field of study will be the moon, stars, and constellations in the night sky. There is much for you to learn about the celestial bodies." Temasah smiled at the concern on Olo's face.

"But now we must rest. Tomorrow we have an important day-- the day you formally become my adopted son." Temasah bid Olo good-night and departed to the lodge next door.

Olo turned on his side. The flap over the smokehole fluttered gently. He pulled Edaw closer to him, and stared into the fire. "I am so glad to be warm... so glad to be safe....so glad to be home...."

CHAPTER 24

OLO AWOKE AS he heard Temasah stomping the slush off his feet. He knew he had just returned from saying his morning prayers. He watched as he threw off his heavy cloak.

Olo sat up and stretched. He rubbed sleep out of his eyes. "Last night I dreamed the bat flew down to me and spoke. It explained to me how my new power should be used. I am to use my wisdom to help people."

Annawa entered with bowls of steaming pine needle tea, hot corn gruel and corn cakes. "Your cheeks are sallow. You must eat to regain your strength," she said.

He hungrily ate the hot food. "May I have more food, Mother?"

"Yes." Annawa heaped more corn gruel in his bowl.

"It is appropriate that you dream so. Today is the last day of your youth. Tomorrow you are a man. A new man with a new name," Temasah said.

"If Nadac is my brother, why does he not live with us? I enjoy his company." Olo reached for another corn cake.

"That is a good idea. I will speak to Nadac's father," Temasah said.

Annawa brought out their fine clothing neatly folded and kept for special occasions. Olo and Temasah dressed in their best. Annawa combed and braided Temasah's hair.

"It is a great honor to wear eagle feathers." Temasah wore his eagle feathers stuck in his top-knot. He inserted the copper spools into his earlobes.

"Today I will wear my father's throat ornament." He produced a shiny, white, mussel shell gorget. On its front, a carved figure, dressed in an elaborate costume, held a war club in one hand and the head of a victim in the other. Temasah wore it around his neck suspended from a bead covered cord.

In his belt he wore an impressive knife with a black obsidian blade, deer antler handle and rawhide wrap at the joint.

Olo recognized that black stone. "I remember my father's cache of prized stone blanks, his trade materials. He used to let me play with the chert blanks he kept in a sack under our sleeping bench. One time I cut my finger on an obsidian arrowhead." Olo held up one finger as he remembered his childhood injury.

Annawa combed Olo's hair. She fashioned a top-knot and decorated it with the eagle feather he had found.

"I will wear my rabbit teeth necklace today," he said.

"Your looks are pleasing to my eyes." She smiled and stood back admiring his looks.

Two guards appeared at the door. "We are to escort you across the plaza and assist your climb up the steps of the temple mound."

Temasah sagged under the weight of a black bearskin robe he pulled on his shoulders. Temasah took the guard's arm in one hand, his cane in the other.

Olo limped with his crutch under one arm. "I will need your help climbing up the stairway," he said to the guard.

"You are the same man who found me and carried me to the village, aren't you?" Olo smiled in recognition.

"Yes, I have been given the privilege of escorting you," the guard said.

All eyes were turned on Olo. He realized he was a member of the village's elite. He was secretly proud. He stood straight and held his head up. *I was a prisoner when I came to this village. Nadac is right. I am lucky.*

"The celebration is in honor of my adoption," he said to the escort.

"Yes, and you will receive a new name and a tattoo," he replied. He smiled at Olo's friendliness.

"Does a tattoo hurt very much? How is it done? Will I bleed? Who will give me the tattoo? Is it painful when the dye is pushed into your skin?"

"Yes, I have heard that it is very painful," he replied.

Olo's eyebrows drew together in a worried expression. "More pain. I can not get away from pain," he sighed.

The sun was warm on their faces as they slowly made their way through the crowds of people. Olo smelled the acrid wood smoke from many fires, and the delicoius smell of venison haunchs being roasted for the feast.

Many traders and visitors had sheltered for the night in hastily built conical huts of willow poles covered with skins and brush. They wove their way around them.

"I see many people using their hands. Is that sign language?" Olo asked.

"Yes, their spoken languages may be different but they all understand a common sign language," he answered.

They stopped at the chunkey yard where many people were watching and betting on the game. The chunkey yard is a hard-packed clay court sunk down in the earth to keep the chunkey stone from rolling out of the court. It is a game where one man rolls a stone disc, a chunkey stone, and both players throw their long, hickory poles at it. The points of the hickory poles are greased with bear grease to make them slippery. Points are scored by hitting the disc, or by coming closest to where it stopped.

"I want to learn to play chunkey! I love to watch the game!" Olo said.

"When your ankle heals," Temasah said.

They continued, maneuvering their way through the throng. The plaza was a maze of craftsmen showing their pottery pieces, or traders showing exotic fur skins, all urging the passersby to see their wares and barter for their goods.

Over the din of the crowd, Olo heard music. He heard shrill wails of a bird-bone whistle and low tones of cane flutes, and the steady beat of drums.

"I see dancers!" he said.

Bowing and swaying, they chanted. With rhythmic and unified step patterns, their movements followed the beat of drums made of pottery-vessels covered tightly with deerskin. Several dancers held hand-sized, pebble-filled rattles. They shook the ornaments, then twisted and turned their bodies, all under the direction of a dance director supervising every move.

"Dancers and singers! I love the festival!"

A dancer suddenly turned and walked on his hands with his feet in the air. He seemed to be dancing just for Olo who clapped his hands in appreciation.

Men dressed in wolf skins howled their wolf clan ceremonial songs. Bird clan men danced in flock formation to honor the arrival of geese, or they hunched in a cluster, then sprang up like a covy of quail. The audience shouted their delight with each dance movement.

Temasah, Olo, and the escorts, found the steps to the great mound and slowly started climbing. As Olo ascended the steps to the temple for his adoption ceremony, a great cheer rose from the crowd. A thrill ran up his spine. "They are cheering for me," he said. He turned and waved with one arm. They cheered even louder.

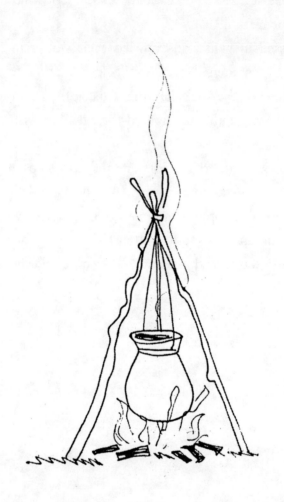

CHAPTER 25

OLO WAS ESCORTED directly into the antechamber of the temple. He grasped Temasah's arm. "Sir, I am worried about being tattooed." He whispered in Temasash's ear. "Do you do it?"

"No, another shaman, an expert tattooer, will do it," Temasah answered softly. "It is a great honor to wear your rank on your forehead. You are marked for life."

"Is it painful?" He looked down at his feet.

"Yes." Temasah placed his hand on Olo's shoulder.

"Remember your ordeal in the depths of the earth and be brave." Temasah entered the main chamber and took his place with the other elders and chiefs.

Olo followed the guard to a small room. The open flap over the smokehole let sunlight flood into the room. He sat on the raised platform and rested his sprained ankle.

Presently, a young shaman entered the room. His face had been tattooed in a black band that reached from ear to ear. His copper ear-spools glinted in the bright light.

He approached. Olo started to stand up. "You may remain seated, since you are injured." He spoke in a kindly voice.

He sprinkled bright, yellow corn meal in Olo's hair and on both his shoulders. Then the shaman held a pipe in his right hand, the stem lifted to the heavens, for the Great Spirit to receive the first draw of the sacred tobacco. He turned east, south, west and north in a complete circle.

"Oh Great Spirit, accept this offering from your servant. Look down and bless us in this endeavor," he prayed.

He offered the pipe to Olo. He took the pipe, placed the bowl in his hand and the stem in his mouth and inhaled deeply. He choked and coughed for several minutes in a coughing frenzy. He could not speak. His throat burned and his eyes watered. He thought his lungs would burst.

When he could finally take a deep breath, he said. "I have never before tasted tobacco."

"Inhale again," the shaman ordered. This time Olo felt a warmth spread through his chest and he began to relax.

"Lie back on the platform," the shaman said. With both hands, Olo picked up his splint, placed his leg on the bed, then lay back. The shaman placed a soft, doeskin pillow under his neck.

"Tattooing provides magical protection against sickness and misfortune. It identifies the wearer's rank or membership in a group. Since you are bird clan, you will have the wings of a blackbird in flight tattooed over your eyebrows." Olo could hear the pride in his voice.

"Just like the tattoo Temasah has?" he asked.

"Yes, exactly like he has," the shaman promised.

He handed Olo a cup of strong, dark tea. "This medicinal tea is made of small pussy willows, whose roots are bruised and crushed, then steeped to make a tea."

Olo drank some of the dark, unpleasant drink. "Ugh." He made a sour face at the bitter taste. It was stronger than Temasah's medicinal tea.

The shaman handed Olo a green stick. "Bite down on this when the pain gets bad."

"Yes, Sir." Shivers ran up his spine.

Olo watched him take an eagle claw out of his medicine bag. "I will describe each procedure if you would like for me to," he said looking into Olo's face.

"Yes, I would like to know what you are doing," Olo said. He felt more relaxed. *I won't be so afraid if I know what you're doing*, he thought.

"First I score the skin on your forehead with this eagle claw. This imparts the power of the bird into your flesh." He pulled the claw across his forehead over his eyebrows.

Olo was unprepared for the pain! He held his breath, with his teeth clamped tight and his mouth shut, but he wanted to scream in pain! Hot tears slid from the corners of his eyes and pooled in his ears. *I am strong. . . I am strong. . .* he thought.

The shaman held up a small wooden mallet and a curved fish jawbone with rows of sharp teeth. "This is the jawbone of a fish with long feelers like a wildcat." He turned the bone to view it from all sides .

"After I puncture your skin with the teeth in the jawbone, I will rub black pigment into the wound. Are you ready?"

"Yes," Olo replied in a little voice, placing the green stick between his teeth.

"Ugh," Olo grunted with each strike the mallet made on the fish jawbone. "Ugh," Olo grunted. *I will look like Temasah with this tattoo. . . I am strong. . . .*

The shaman introduced the black pigment through the ruptures in the forehead skin. With a soft doeskin he wiped away the blood that seeped out of the wounds.

Olo gritted his teeth with the pain but he did not cry out. *I fear pain. This is almost as painful as being cold, wet and hungry in the blackness of the cave*, he thought.

Again and again the shaman pierced Olo's skin and rubbed in the black dye. Each small incision bled. The blood was wiped away with a soft doeskin dipped in water. The smell of blood made him gag.

How much longer must I endure this pain? I must act like a man--I must not cry out. Olo remained stoic but his thoughts raged on.

"Drink the rest of your medicinal tea Olo," the shaman said.

"I feel light-headed," Olo confided.

"Yes, the smoke and the tea cause that," the young shaman said. Held up a soot stained finger. "The pigment is made from soot. Oil is burned in a round clay pot with a small opening and is collected from the inside of the pot."

"Will it wear off my skin?" Olo asked.

"No, this tattoo is forever. It will never wash or wear off. It says bird clan for the rest of your life. It is a mark of distinction," the shaman said proudly.

That was the last word Olo remembered. Suddenly he was awake. Olo staggered to his feet, in pain, breathless. His brow furrowed. "What is wrong?" he asked.

But instead of feeling joyful he suddenly felt almost alarmed. He sank down again on the bed, too dizzy to stand up.

"I can hardly open my eyes!" He squinted through slits. Feeling his forehead with his hand, he remembered his new tattoo. He tried not to wrinkle his brow.

"My forehead is swollen and my eyes are almost swollen shut. I must have dozed off. I must have fallen asleep."

"Yes, you did," the shaman said coming into the room. "Let the medicine wear off while I pierce your earlobes."

"Pierce my ears?" Olo asked in alarm.

"Wouldn't you like to wear copper ear spools?"

"Yes, but...." Olo felt confused.

The shaman reached for a small ceremonial piercing tool. Olo hardly felt the pricks in his earlobes. The shaman inserted the small copper earspools and wiped away the blood.

"Now you wear emblems of your rank. I gave you a black tattoo over your eyebrows in the shape of a soaring bird with outstretched wings," the shaman said proudly.

"Yes, thank you." Olo agreed, but all he could think about was his painfully swollen forehead, the blood that seeped from the tattoo, and his sore earlobes.

CHAPTER 26

THE SUN WAS only a hand's width from the western edge of the sky when Olo was summoned to the main chamber. The young shaman led him down the corridor where they were told to wait just outside the big chamber.

In the distance, he heard the boom of a pot drum and the faint wails of flute music.

The scent of spiced hickory oil mixed with tobacco and wood smoke seeped under the brightly painted door flap.

He heard the chief give ritual thanks for everything in earth and sky. "This prayer is so all-inclusive, it has lasted for hours," the young shaman said.

The prayer droned in Olo's ears. Then he heard the chief say, "Nadac, your courageous deed has been noted by the council members here convened. When spirits of the cave wanted to eat Olo, you snatched him back from the jaws of death. Storytellers will tell of your bravery in the history of our village."

The chief spoke louder. "Nadac, you are a young man ready to accept the responsibility of providing for and protecting our village. Your honorary name has been chosen. Nadomas, from this day forward, everyone will address you by this new name, Nadomas."

After a few minutes, a guard held open the door flap and bid Olo and the shaman enter. A puff of wind entered the chamber. The wicks in the firebowls hissed and the light wavered. In the flickering light, the painted images on the walls seemed to move and shift uneasily.

"My head is still dizzy," Olo said. The shaman steadied him.

Olo stood before the high chief. He noticed the council members had donned the trappings of rank and power. The high chief wore a copper breast plate embossed with images of mythical bird men. Many wore necklaces of beads carved from mussel-shells.

The room fell silent when the chief began to speak. His deep voice filled the room.

"A worm on a branch came to us. We fed the creature, gave him a safe home. We were patient while he matured, then one day he became a thing of beauty--a butterfly."

The chief flung his arms open for emphasis while speaking. "Things are not always as they seem to be. A fat leaf can change into a butterfly ready to fly away. A cocoon has to split open to let out the new. As worms change and take flight, so have you." The chief looked directly at Olo.

Olo looked at him and tried to understand the meaning of his words.

The chief raised his hands. "This big mound, a powerful place, started as a pebble, then a handful of dirt. It grew into a powerful place, just as you will grow into a powerful person."

Olo looked at him, eyes wide and listened intently.

Temasah stepped forward and stood beside Olo. Temasah turned toward Olo. He lay both hands on Olo's shoulders.

"Adoption is a sacred bond never to be broken. I choose you to be my blood and my flesh. You are first in my eyes and first in my heart. You are my son."

Olo felt the thin shoulder blades under Temasah's tunic as they embraced. Both of them had tears in their eyes, but neither spoke. The looks they exchanged were full of love.

The chief raised the carved wooden staff in his hand. "Greetings, Olo. This is the last time you will be greeted by the name your umbilical cord-cutting mother gave to you. Your deeds have earned you a new name, Olosah. After this ceremony, you will, for the rest of your life, be called Olosah."

The chief banged the staff three times. A man came forward and handed him a small bag. "Corn meal connects the past, present, and future."

He held his hand out. Olosah took the bag. "Thank you, Sir," he said.

The chief banged the staff again. A second man approached the chief and handed him a cup. "This cup has a ceremonial purpose. You will one day be invited to the drink ritual beverage known as the 'black drink.' This cup is yours to use at that ceremonial occasion."

Olosah accepted the cup. The large shell cup was engraved with a figure in ceremonial regalia, holding a staff laden with tied mythical creatures.

"Thank you," Olosah said and bowed formally.

The chief continued in a stern voice. "The purpose of the festival, with ritual songs and dances, is to bring back to mind and heart everything that gives the people their roots on earth."

He banged the wooden staff three more times. "This meeting is adjourned. Let us join the festivities."

Darkness had fallen when they went outside and the air was heavy laden with smoke from the bonfires.

The guards escorted Temasah and Olosah down the steps of the mound. Nadomas waited there to greet them.

"Congratulations, Olo, er, I mean, Olosah." He looked at the bloody tattoo. "Was it painful?" he asked.

"Yes, it was." Olosah looked at him through swollen eyelids.

He clapped his arm around Nadomas's shoulders. "I have missed you. Will you live with us?" Olosah asked looking at Temasah.

"Yes, he has permission to live with us and learn with you." Temasah smiled.

"Good," Olosah said. He had forgotten the pain in his forehead.

The central plaza was full of people. There were bonfires to light up the night. Music, singing and dancing groups were surrounded by crowds of on-lookers.

The scent of roasting venison wafted on the air. "I am hungry." Olosah hobbled toward a haunch of venison roasting over a fire. Temasah and Nadomas followed.

When the cook saw the new tattoo, he said, "Be my guest. Eat your fill. It is my honor to feed you." He cut slices of juicy meat. " I am proud to be feeding the guest of honor and his family."

Olosah and Nadomas were offered corn cakes. They ate hungrily.

A drum began throbbing. The dancers were starting again. The drums began, low at first, then rising to boom like thunder. Now the tempo of the dance picked up and the dancers swayed back and forth before a circle of men and women formed around the bonfire. They circled the fire several times in a shuffling step dance. Then they broke into a stomp dance accompanied by drum and flute.

"Nadomas, I am excited to see so many new things."

"Yes, this is my first festival," Nadomas said.

Laughing and teasing, a group of singers and musicians recognized Olosah and his party. Playfully they surrounded them and began singing to them. Accompanied by flute music the singers intoned their songs which they had learned by heart.

"It looks difficult," Olosah said as he watched one musician place his fingers over holes in his flute and blow into it to make sounds.

"His fingers move fast," Nadomas said in wonder.

Another musician played a panpipe made of bone. All the singers had rattles made of turtle shells or gourds and many shook clapper rattles in time with the drum beats. Some of the dancers had turtle-shell rattles strapped onto their legs so that each step added to the rhythm.

Olosah leaned down and spoke into Nadomas's ear, "The girls are beautiful, don't you agree? Look at that tall girl with her long hair swinging. She is the most beautiful girl I have ever seen."

Nadomas nodded. "Yes," he said, then blushed and looked down at his feet.

Young girls, dressed in their finest clothes, sang and danced around the bonfire. One of the dancers raised her arms like birds in flight. Her head was lowered. Her feet touched the ground toe first, then tapped the foot, tap-step-tap-step. All eyes were on the beautiful, young dancer twirling around and around as she danced.

Suddenly a cry went up! The music and dancing stopped. Everyone looked around in confusion! What was the problem?

Someone pointed upward. There arose a shout, then a collective cry of amazement!

Up there, above the burning embers that drifted up into the night sky, a burst of color slowly faded. The sky began to shimmer with bursts of color: red, yellow, blue appeared as a flash, then faded, only to appear again in another part of the night sky.

An undulating splendor of colored lights in the northern sky flashed, then faded and disappeared. Again and again the celestial lights filled the sky with the glittering shower.

"Oh, look at the lights in the sky!" Olosah cried.

Everyone shouted "Ahhhhhh". . . "Ohhhhhhh." People were amazed. They stood in awe of the lights in the northern sky.

"They look like bright spiders dancing in the sky!" Olosah cried.

Then a roar went up from the crowd assembled there. Temasah held up his hands. When the were quiet, he said, "The Great Spirit has honored Olosah this time by sending the bright, shimmering colors to light up the night sky. It is a spirit message of hope. It confirms Olosah as a future leader of his people! One message was sent from his clan totem, the eagle, and this message from the Great Spirit in the sky!"

Everyone cheered and called his name. Hot, happy tears streamed down his face. He hugged Temasah and Nadomas. "In my new village, I have found a new life with my new family. My heart is filled with happiness."

Olosah's name was on everyone's lips. A shout went up from the crowd, Olosah! Olosah! Olosah!

BIBLIOGRAPHY

"Aurora Borealis." *Encyclopedia Britannica.* 1967 ed.

"A Wing and a Prayer." *Jacksonville Times-Union* May 11, 1996: p.D-3

Bierhorst, John. *Myths & Tales of the American Indians.* New York: Indian Head Books, 1976

Brian, Jeffrey P. "The Great Mound Robbery." *Archaeology* May/June 1988: 19-25.

Brown, Robin C., *Florida's First People.* Florida: Pineapple Press, Inc., 1994.

Brown, Vinson. *Return of the Indian Spirit.* California" CelestialArts, 1981.

Bryant, Page. "The Forgotten Monuments: The Sacred Mounds of Turtle Island." *Wildfire* Fall 1996: 18-21.

Clottes, Jean and Jean Courtin. "Stone Age Gallery by the Sea." *Archaeology* May/June 1993: 40-43.

Eckert, Allen W. *The Frontiersmen*. New York" Bantam Books, 1970.

Fagan, Brian. "Paleolithic Masterpieces." *Archaeology* July/August 1996: 69-72.

Fagan, Brian. "Teaching New Dogs Old Tricks." *Archaeology* November/December 1994: 12-14.

French, Barbara. Personal Communication Bat Conservation International, Inc., 16 October, 1996.

Fundaburk, Emma Lila. *Southwestern Indians Life Portraits*. Florida: Rose Printing Co., 1958.

Guitar, Dr. Barry and Dr. Edward G. Conture. *If You Think Your Child is Stuttering*. Stuttering Fondation of America: 1997.

Hantman, Jeffrey L. and Gary Dunham. "The Enlightened Archaeologist." *Archaeology* May/June 1993: 44-49.

Hausman, Gerald. *Tunkashila*. New York: St. Martin's Press, 1992.

Hausman, Gerald. *Turtle Island Alphabet*. New York: St. Martin's Press, 1993.

Healy, Paul F. "Music of the Maya." *Archaeology* January/February 1988: 25-31.

Hicks, Ronald, ed. *Native American Culture in Indiana*. Indiana: The Minnetrista Cultural Center, 1992.

Iseminger, William R. "Mighty Cahokia." *Archaeology* May/June 1996: 31-37.

Josephy, Alvin M. Jr., ed. *America in 1492*. New York: First Vintage Books, 1993.

Josephy, Alvin M. Jr., ed. *The Indian Heritage of America*. Boston: Houghton Mifflin Co., 1991.

Kane, Sharyn and Richard Keeton. *Beneath These Waters*. Georgia: National Park Service, 1993.

Kelsey, Morton. *Dreamquest*. Massachusetts: Element, 1992.

Kellar, James H. *An Introduction to the Prehistory of Indiana*. Indiana: Indiana Historical Society, 1983.

Kelly, Kim. "The Early Middle Woodland in the Upper Great Lakes." *Indian Artifact Magazine* February 1995: 12-14

Krensky, Stephen. *Children of the Earth and Sky*. New York: Scholastic Inc., 1991.

Land, Doug. "Archeomicrobiotic Fingerprinting of Red Ochre and Early Paleoindian." *Indian Artifact Magazine* August 1995: 27

Lysek, Carol Ann. "Archaeologists May Overlook Value of Fiber Artifacts." *The Mammoth Trumpet* March, 1997: 18-20.

Maestro, Betsy and Giulio. *The Discovery of the Americas*. New York: Mulberry Books, 1991.

Morris, Ramona and Desmond. *Men and Snakes*. New York: McGraw-Hill, 1965.

Marshack, Alexander. "Images of the Ice Age." *Archaeology* July/August 1995: 29-39.

McDonald, Jerry N. and Susan L. Woodward. *Indian Mounds of the Atlantic Coast*. Newark, Ohio: McDonald & Woodward Publishing Co., 1987.

Mehringer, Peter J., Jr., "Weapons of Ancient Americans." *National Geographic* October, 1988: 500-503.

Milanich, Jerald T. and Samuel Proctor. *Tacachale*. Florida: Florida University Press, 1994.

Milanich, Jerald T., ed. *The Florida Anthropologist*. Volume 31, Number 4 December 1978.

"Monarchs: A Multinational Asset." *National Geographic* October, 1988: 29.

Parker, Arthur C. *The Indian How Book*. New York: Dover Publications, Inc., 1975.

Phillips, John Franklin. *The American Indian in Alabama and the Southeast*. Tennessee: United Methodist Publishing House, 1986.

"Reptile." *Encyclopedia Britannica*. 1967 ed.

Rigaud, Jean-Phillippe, "Lascaux Cave." *National Geographic* October, 1988: 482-499.

Scarry, Margaret C., ed. *Foraging and Farming in the Eastern Woodlands*. Florida: University Press of Florida, 1993.

Smith-Barzini, Marlene and Howard Egger-Bovet. *US Kids History: Book of the American Indians*. New York: Little, Brown and Company, 1994.

Soffer, Olga, Pamela Vandiver, Martin Oliva, and Ludik Seitl. "Case of the Exploding Figurines." *Archaeology* January/February 1993: 36-39.

Speight, Charlotte F. *Hands in Clay*. California: Mayfield Publishing Co., 1989.

Stuart, George E. "Etowah." *National Geographic* October, 1991: 54-67.

Turner, Geoffrey. *Indians of North America*. New York: Sterling Publishing Co. 1992.

Tuttle, Merlin D. "Saving North America's Beleaguered Bats." *National Geographic*. August 1995: 37-57.

Wallace, Black Elk, and William S. Lyon. *Black Elk*. California: HarperSanFrancisco, 1991.

Weatherford, Jack. *Native Roots*. New York: Fawcett Columbine, 1991.

Zitkala-Sa, *Old Indian Legends*. Nebraska: University of Nebraska Press, 1985.

CHAPTER BY CHAPTER

The Mississippian era flourished from roughly A.D. 700 to A.D. 1500. During that time of peace and prosperity, a sophisticated culture thrived and the largest earthen structures in North America were built.

Olo has seen thirteen winters. Tall and thin, he stutters badly. When he sees enemy warriors approaching he cries, "L-Look! E-Enemy." The workers only look at him and laugh.

Nadac, a short, angry boy about the same age, is in the raiding party and captures Olo. When Olo catches the eagle's food and is proclaimed a "chosen one," Nadac is jealous. At every turn, he teases and taunts Olo.

Chapter 1

While harvesting tobacco, Olo and the workers are attacked by hostile warriors. After a fierce struggle, Olo is captured by the short, angry warrior, Nadac. The captives are tied together with ropes around their necks, and forced to carry their tobacco bundles on their backs. On a well-worn path through the woods, they are forced west. When the path opens, Olo gets his first glimpse of the mounds on the distant horizon.

VOCABULARY: pyramid, hostile

Chapter 2

The warriors march their captives across an open field. Olo is awed by the sight of the huge mounds. From the sky, an eagle drops its prey, a rabbit, and Olo catches it. This action causes much excitement. The guards consider this an omen, since they are bird clan and the eagle is their totem. They agree, Olo is a "chosen one." Olo is separated from the other captives. Led up the steps of the great mound, he waits with fear and trepidation outside the council house.

VOCABULARY: conical, palasade, omen, chert, effigies, plaza

Chapter 3

Summoned before the chiefs and elders of the tribe, Olo listens as the guard tells the story. Much discussion follows. Then a hush comes over the room as the elderly shaman, Temasah enters. He asks them to share his vision. In a trance he sees the copper mask of the long-nosed-god, then Olo's face. After the trance he asks the council for Olo to be placed in his care as an apprentice shaman. The council agrees.

VOCABULARY: gorget, shaman, grimace, apprentice

Chapter 4

Olo accompanies Temasah to his lodge where he is greeted by Edaw, the white dog, and Temasah's wife, Annawa. Olo is told the legend of the white dog. Edaw sniffs him, then lays down in total submission at Olo's feet, more proof that Olo is a "chosen one." Olo stutters and Temasah wonders if the spirit working in Olo causes him to stutter. Annawa brings food. Safe and well fed, Olo sleeps peacefully that night.

VOCABULARY: submission, sacrifice, vessels

Chapter 5

The next day after breakfast and morning prayers, Temasah explains the routine. Olo hears shamanic lessons in the morning and works in the afternoon. Everyone in the tribe must work. Annawa teaches Olo to make a rawhide harness for Edaw, so he can pull a travois loaded with fresh drinking water to the mound builders. As they work, Nadac teases Olo for stuttering and doing woman's work. That night, Olo is troubled because he stutters. The shaman advises Olo, "Take a deep breath, then speak your mind."

VOCABULARY: potions, frail, decrepit, travois, burdened, pallet

Chapter 6

The day's shamanic lesson surprises Olo. He is given a fat worm on a branch and told to observe it. Olo reveals his sad history. His father never returned from a trading trip, and his mother died of the coughing sickness. Olo did not speak for ten moons. When he spoke again, he stuttered. Adopted by a large family who teased him for stuttering and often beat him, Olo says he will not be missed.

VOCABULARY: crevice, humiliation, recetpacle, taunt

Chapter 7

Ten to twelve days pass. Olo notices the worm's case split open and a butterfly emerges. Together he and Tomasah release the butterfly so it can work for mother earth. Olo delivers drinking water to the hard working mound builders. They explain how the mound is built, one basketfull of earth at a time, stomped hard and packed down with their feet. On the way home, he stops to watch a chunkey game. Nadac taunts him in front of the crowd. Embarrassed, Olo again wonders why Nadac hates him. What can he do to put a stop to his taunts?

VOCABULARY: sensed, quivered, embarrassment

Chapter 8

Bad weather keeps Olo at his lesson where the old Temasah reveals the healing power of roots, leaves, bark, and how to use them. He reveals many shamanic secrets. Olo is sworn to secrecy. He promises never to reveal the shaman's psychic surgery techniques.

VOCABULARY: lament, vertical, girdle, clapper rattle

Chapter 9

Annawa requires Olo's assistance at the potter's lodge. She reveals the secret of exploding pottery figurines. She tells Olo how to make them and when to use them. Olo grinds ancient pottery shards into powder so she can mix the spirits of the old pots into the spirits of the new pots. She asks Olo and Edaw to go to the woods and bring back a load of wood.

VOCABULARY: beconed, explode, figurine, shatters, loess, coils, temper, potshards, hoisted

Chapter 10

On the way back, Nadac attacks them. Olo, in anger for the first time, fights back. A fierce fight ensues. Olo looks up to see the crowd that has gathered around them. This gives Nadac his opportunity. He hits Olo in the head with a rock. Olo is taking a beating, when Edaw leaps onto Nadac, bites him, and breaks up the fight. Nadac runs away bloody and defeated.

VOCABULARY: hackles, gouged, dispersing. kiln

Chapter 11

Olo limps back to the shaman's lodge. After his wounds are treated, he expresses anger and frustration with Nadac's continuing hostility. Temasah wisely advises Olo that life always shifts from harmony to struggle. He tells Olo he will be a better shaman for knowing pain, suffering, and heartache. Olo falls asleep with Edaw's head nuzzled under his hand as Temasah sings a song of healing.

VOCABULARY: assessing, sassafrass, savage, harmony, incantations

Chapter 12

    The next morning, full of pain, Olo must hold his head high as he helps Annawa fire her pots and pipes in an open firing. Olo wonders if people are laughing at his misfortune, or happy to see him. Olo helps control the ring of fire that slowly burns inward so the pots warm slowly.

    Next day, after the pots have cooled, Annawa presents Olo with an effigy pipe made in Edaw's image. Olo is surprised that he will be allowed to smoke at ceremonial occasions. He has many doubts and questions about becoming a man, but keeps them in his heart.

VOCABULARY: compressed, spiral, radiated, subjecting

Chapter 13

    Several weeks pass. Winter's approach quickens the pace of daily life at the village. Temasah hurries to collect bark for medicinal teas. Olo nearly steps on a copper-colored snake. Olo wants to kill it but Temasah warns that snakes are messengers from the underground, and killing a snake brings trouble and danger into your life.

    That afternoon, as Olo and Edaw return from delivering drinking water to the mound builders, he sees a crowd gathered at the river bank watching dugout canoe races. An accident spills the boys into the flood swollen river. Olo, without hesitation, dives into the water and saves one of the boys. It is Nadac.

VOCABULARY: granaries, pemmican, wafted, antler hoe, deadfall, boneset, prickly ash, dugout canoe, retched

Chapter 14

Olo orders the unconscious Nadac to be placed on the travois, and taken to the shaman's healing lodge. Temasah treats Nadac's wound. Before he regains consciousness, Temasah prays for the Great Spirit to heal the wound in Nadac's heart that causes him to walk with evil. Temasah tells Nadac that he is in a place between the Great Spirit and earth. He must choose where he wants to be. When Nadac recovers, he asks Olo why he saved him. Olo answers the Great Spirit ordered him to do it.

VOCABULARY: trance, visions

Chapter 15

With great ceremony the tribal elders meet in the council house to acknowledge Olo's heroic deed. Temasah dresses in his finest robe, his shell gorget around his neck, and copper spools in his earlobes. Annawa presents Olo with new doeskin tunic and leggins. Olo has never had such fine clothes. For good luck, Annawa gives Olo the rabbit's teeth made into a necklace. Together Olo and Temasah go to the council meeting. It is decided Olo will go on a vision quest to face his fears and prove he is worthy of adoption into the tribe and brave enough to become Temasah's son.

VOCABULARY: dignity, tunic, shamanic, elite, pestles, mortars, vision quest, ointment, extricate, habitation, invocation

Chapter 16

Olo prepares to go on the vision quest, first confiding he is afraid of darkness, bats, and snakes. Temasah shows Olo the snake tattoo that starts in a spiral on his stomach and curls between his old, sagging breasts. He tells Olo snakes bring down rain from the sky to water the corn. Snakes are powerful and should be honored.

Temasah advises Olo about the dangers he will face in the cave. Olo is to find the red spiral Temasah made years earlier, make his own spiral beside it, then dedicate himself to the underground spirits in the cave. He must ask their blessing before he can become a shaman.

VOCABULARY: scurried, urgently, retreating, impede, morsels, pelt, quiver, fetch

Chapter 17

Temasah advises Olo his vision quest will be seven sleeps of isolation to face his fears, find his personal toten and find his spirit voice. Temasah gives Olo a piece of doeskin. He tells Olo to tie it on his belt. When Olo asks what it is for, Temasah replies he will know when the time comes.

Annawa hears an owl hooting in the night and fears for Olo's safety. Edaw wants to accompany Olo. Temasah has to hold Edaw while Olo departs. Olo hears Edaw's howls of disappointment as he walks out the pallisade gate. Olo enters the woods on a path of his own choosing. He walks through the woods until black storm clouds force him to make camp for the night.

VOCABULARY: anticipation, intaglio, red ochre, isolation, portent, broused, ratcheted, eerie

Chapter 18

Following the path beside the river, Olo cuts reeds for torches. Olo freezes in mid-step as he watches snakes writhe and slither on top of each other entering a crack in a rock outcropping. The path seems to end at the base of a limestone bluff. Olo sees the entrance to the cave, a black hole in the cliff. He makes a log lean-to and camps for the might. Before retiring, Olo prays for a clean heart and spirit ready to receive messages.

VOCABULARY: impede, copse

Chapter 19

At dawn the next morning, Olo greets the rising sun with a prayer to guide his footsteps. Stashing his rope and pemmican, he walks to the bluff and climbs up the boulders. Lighting a reed torch, Olo wriggles through the narrow entrance to the cave. He finds himself enveloped in the stench of bat guano. He hurries out of the cave. Realizing the reason for the doeskin Temasah gave him, he ties it over his mouth and nose and re-enters the cave. Bats rustle and shift position overhead, raining urine down on him. An infant bat is frightened into letting go of its mother and perishes in the beetle filled guano. He hurries through corridors that open on a vast cavern where a frozen waterfall glistens like moonlight on snow. Awed by the beauty of the cave, Olo sees markings on the cave walls made by earlier visitors. He finds the spiral, carves his own spiral, colors it with red ocher, then dedicates it to the underground spirits.

VOCABULARY: homage, spiral intaglio, vaulted, tranquility, guano, stench, dedicate

Chapter 20

Olo's torch burns low. As he scurries toward the exit, a rock ledge crumbles and he plunges into frigid water. In inky blackness, he swims frantically, until his hand touches a rock ledge and climbs to safety. His ankle is injured. Olo is trapped in the bowels of the cave; cold, wet, and hungry. He prays, but the hopelessness of the situation overwhelms him. He screams and sobs. Time passes. Olo realizes this is a cruel test but he must hold out. Olo sings the song of lament for the dead.

Slowly a light appears on the cavern ceiling, walls, and shines on the water. Nadac calls to Olo.. He has come to save him. Nadac throws a rope to Olo and pulls him to safety. As they exit the cave, Olo picks up the infant bat skull for his personal totem.

VOCABULARY: garbled, wrenching, fatigue. sodden

Chapter 21

Looking down from the cave entrance, Olo sees Edaw tied to a tree, barking with excitement. Nadac helps Olo stumble to the camp, where he peals off Olo's sodden clothing and rubs warmth into his skin with clumps of deer moss. Olo falls into an exhausted sleep.

He awakes to find Nadac roasting venison over a big camp fire. Nadac hands the roasted liver to Olo. Nadac explains how Temasah found him, told him Olo was in danger, and gave him Edaw to sniff out the trail. Olo thanks Nadac for saving his life.

Next morning, Nadac finds a branched sappling and makes a crutch. Then he wraps a piece of fur around Olo's sprained ankle and fashions a splint of sticks tied with rope. They spend the day resting and eating. In conversation they resolve their differences. Nadac notices Olo no longer stutters.

VOCABULARY: reinforced, quavering, talisman, gorget, immobilize, foretell

Chapter 22

The next morning they awake to hushed silence. An early snowfall covers them. With the crutch under one arm and Nadac under the other, Olo slips and slides through the snow. They move slowly as Olo is cold and in pain.

Nadac knows a way to get Olo warm. He hunts for white oak bark, makes a fire in a hole in the ground for Olo to sit over with his blanket capturing the heat. They spend a fitfull night.

Next morning they encounter a hunting party and are recognized immediately. Their story is told and re-rold every night around lodge fires. One of the hunters carries Olo on his back to the mound village.

VOCABULARY: exhilarated, disorder, chaos, smoldering, draught

Chapter 23

Olo is carried to the shaman's healing lodge where Temasah offers a prayer of thanksgiving for their return. Olo asks for corn cakes and hickory nut butter. Temasah wants to hear about everything Olo saw, heard and experienced on his vision quest. The day is spent in conversation. Temasah notices Olo does not stutter.

Temasah presents Olo with a new medicine bundle for the tiny, bat skull. Olo goes to sleep that night thankful to be safe at home.

VOCABULARY: procession, cruel, discussion, aspect

Chapter 24

In Olo's dream, a bat flies down to him and explains how his new powers should be used to help people. Temasah says the dream is appropriate since this is the last day of his youth. Tomorrow, when he is adopted, he will be a new man with a tattoo and a new name.

Preparations for the celebration begin. There will be quantities of food. Games and contests are planned. Merchants plan to attend the festival to sell their wares. Musicians with their musical instruments are summoned. There will be stomp dances around a huge bonfire held in the plaza in front of the Great Mound. Everyone is excited about the festival.

VOCABULARY: corn gruel, obsidian, cache, escorting, elite, acrid, conical, maneuvering, throng, exotic, covy

Chapter 25

The council house atop the Great Mound is filled with chiefs, elders and shamen, all dressed in their finest robes, feathers, and ear spools. In honor of his brave deed, Olo receives his first tattoo, a bird in flight over his eyebrows, just like Temasah's tattoo. Olo is adopted into the tribe as the son of their greatest shaman, and re-named, Olosah.

For saving Olo's life in the cave, Nadac is re-named, Nadomas, to honor Olo and Temasah. Nadac's change of heart brought out a sensitive, caring person who is eager to please and happy to be Olosah's friend. He will live in the lodge with Temasah and Olosah.

VOCABULARY: antechanber, medicinal, mallet, puncture, pigment, ruptures, soot, distinctive, emblems

Chapter 26

After a night of singing, stomp dancing and merriment, as the bonfire dies down, someone shouts! Up in the sky is an aurora borealis! All the chiefs and elders are awed by the display in the northern night sky. The flashing, shimmering lights say the Great Spirit is pleased with Olosah and Nadomas. The two boys face the future as friends and brothers. Olosah gives thanks to the Great Spirit for helping him control his stuttering, and for giving him a happy home. Olosah has a new father, mother, brother, and loving dog. "My heart is filled with happiness," Olo says.

VOCABULARY: corridor, all-inclusive, droned, mythical, umbilical cord, adjourned, panpipe, undulating, celestial

ABOUT THE AUTHOR

Jo Ann Harter was born in Rockport, Indiana, not far from Angel Mounds. Angel Mounds State Historic Site, located on the banks of the Ohio River, is one of the best-preserved prehistoric Native American settlements in the United States. She has had a life-long interest in Native Americans, the Mound Builders in particular. While doing historical research at the University of Illinois, she attended a lecture by the author, Dee Alexander Brown, and the idea for *Olo of the Mound Builders* was conceived. She polished the story to perfection on her three children and later three grandchildren.

Printed in the United States
113389LV00003B/7-21/A